"Extremely readable and undeniably creative,
My Dear Watson *should be on your bookshelf*
if you have even a passing interest in Sherlock Holmes."
Out in Print

"My Dear Watson *is a great addition*
to the hundreds of spinoffs to the Sherlock canon..."
The Rainbow Round Table of the ALA

"Mrs. Watson: Untold Stories *puts real history into a*
dramatic fictional frame. Mrs. Watson herself is funny—
dry yet personable."
Tyson Kadwell, co-author of *Gay A Day*

"I was as ensnared as Mrs. Watson by the queer secret
history of many revered writers—and a few kings, queens,
and composers, for good measure—whose legacies L.A.
Fields explores with lovely prose and sharp-eyed wit. Mrs.
Watson: Untold Stories *is a bittersweet delight."*
Alyssa Wees, author of *The Waking Forest*

Published by Lethe Press
lethepressbooks.com
Copyright © L.A. Fields 2021

ISBN: 978-1-59021-440-4

Cover illustration: Ben Baldwin
Typesetting: Ryan Vance

Mrs. Watson
Untold Stories

L.A. Fields

The Nightmare Pygmalion

Interesting news: I'm going to Australia this fall! I want to go, and I know I'll be happy about it when the weather turns, when we're sailing away, when (if) I see a kangaroo, but the circumstances surrounding this exotic vacation are... well, they involve Sherlock Holmes, and there's no getting around that. There will be no getting away from him on a boat, either, but that's a complaint for another day.

I don't know what business Holmes has in Australia. I could speculate a half a dozen things, but I won't ask. Perhaps his doctor has told him to get out of the damp of England for his health (he is sixty-seven years old, and not as impervious as he'd like to be), perhaps it's something to do with his bees (maybe a bee symposium, or a bee colleague with a strange new monstrous bee specimen to show him), or maybe he just wants to see Australia, and would like to take Watson with him. He didn't mean to invite me any more than I meant to jump on the boat with them, but Watson... he wants to bring everyone to the land down under. He accepted Holmes's invitation, and then turned around and issued one to me as if it was his idea for he and I alone. That's how Holmes and I found ourselves agreeing to one big family vacation together, when we always prefer to keep out of each other's sphere: we each thought we were signing on to have Watson to ourselves. Now we'll have to share him.

Depending on which city, which climate we're headed to, I'll try to plan my own activities. I've never been to Australia—if we're on the beach, I'll enjoy the beach, and if we're in the bush, I'll explore the bush. Mountains? I will climb. Metropolis? I will shop. I'll give Watson clear windows of time away from me, so that Holmes won't have to be jealous of my evenings, because he and Watson will have some days for themselves. I am a gracious wife, a generous wife, and rather than choose my battles, I opt for tactical retreats, when I have ground to cede.

I'm resolved to be happy about this until something (someone) comes to stop me.

September 9th 1921

We'll be setting sail within the week, weather depending. I say 'sail' but the concern isn't the wind on a steam ship, so much as the chops the wind creates. I've seen pictures of the boat we'll be on: our ocean liner the SS Osterley, which will take us from London direct to Brisbane, through the Atlantic, the Suez Canal, then the Pacific, right to the east coast of Australia. It's quite a bit grander than the ship that took me to America for my schooling, some forty-odd years ago. The Osterley has two smoke stacks on it, and Watson and I will have a room separate from Holmes, who I believe has secured one of the smaller rooms on the boat for himself, just to prove how ascetic he is, perhaps. There's no reason to be stingy on the back end of life—there are only so many vacations left for all of us, though quite a few more for me as I'm not yet fifty. Nevertheless, Holmes will probably spend most of his time on deck, spying everyone's secrets based on the wear of their shoes—it's no matter to me. I'll spend my days in the library or lounging in the chill ocean air, we really won't have to interact for the month or so that we'll be on that boat, if I'm lucky. Let Watson run messages between us if he must, and let him sit between us at dinner saying the same little aside once to one of us, and again to the other. He'll be, as Robert Frost might call it, a mending wall.

Holmes has come to stay near us, so that we can all three depart for London and the shipyard together. He also took it upon his gracious self to offer us packing advice for the climate (while it's winter here it's summer down under) and the terrain (not that he's ever been, but of course his guess is always better than ours). Watson takes even his criticism like praise from Caesar. When Holmes came to my suitcases, however, he started pulling out the things he found impractical for such a wild continent and dropping them on the floor. I was about to start calling him foul names, but Watson came through first to pick up the things Holmes threw down; I would not bend to fetch them, and Holmes most likely would not have been shamed into cleaning up his own mess, so it was Watson who did it to avoid upsetting the honor of both proud parties. He put my things on the back of my vanity's chair, giving Holmes a look that said, *Let's try that again, shall we?* and myself a look that said, *Don't let him bother you, it's only what he wants.* I believe my dear Watson could stop a dog fight without being bitten, I truly do.

I probably won't write again until the voyage is underway—until then.

September 15th 1921

Well, we're settled in on the Osterley now. The energy on this ship is more than I expected—I'm going on a vacation of sorts, but a lot of the other passengers are emigrating to Australia for work. There were tears and desperate hugs from those staying to those leaving, and a fearful sort of tension has remained for days after casting off and getting underway; some of these people may never see England again. Their children will be Australian from now on. Their home is a place they've never been before. It's an optimistic sort of terror that I'm only experiencing from the outside, as an observer. I feel as aloof as Holmes himself, watching these people and wondering at their journeys.

I have begun making friends with the other married ladies, most of them younger than me. There are plenty of newlyweds, off with their boys to find their fortune in a new land. Watson has become such a fan of our captain that he seems to be matchmaking between that man and Holmes, securing an invitation for Holmes to the captain's table that Holmes did not want, and only endured long enough to insist that his identity is not to be spread about this boat while he is on it. He doesn't want to be bombarded by working-class fans of my husband's stories, you see. He has made a companion of his own, someone so seedy-looking that when I spot them walking shoulder-to-shoulder about the deck, conversing stoically, I wonder if that man isn't the reason we're all on this boat to begin with. Perhaps that man is a criminal he needs to interrogate or capture? Maybe that fellow and the captain are running some smuggling operation, and that is why Holmes wanted to avoid the captain? Or maybe that is precisely why he allowed Watson to go bumbling around telling his secrets, because he's playing an intricate chess game with these men? Or nothing is going on, and Holmes has befriended the one person who won't want to chatter his ear off, who knows?

Watson and I have been married long enough that I'm starting to think like him, with his stories and speculations. When that idea occurred to me I couldn't help but smile about it. If sharing his madness is the price of his company, I'll pay it without complaint. I'll consider it a part of *folie à deux* dues, that's fine with me.

October 17th 1921

I've been in such a fog on this boat; so little happens differently day-to-day that it's like a stint in purgatory. Every day is so much the same that the calendar becomes meaningless, but it looks like tomorrow is the day it ends, or so the captain has announced. He recommended at dinner tonight that we all pack our things and double-check our papers for disembarkment, in case the weather is in our favor. I assume I'll be as jelly-legged as a fawn when I step onto land again, it's been so long.

October 22nd 1921

At last: some peace has been found. Our station for the next few weeks is comfortable, near the beach, which mesmerizes me, as it's the ocean at the end of the world as far as I'm concerned. We're at the Breakfast Creek Hotel, right on the Brisbane River, and by 'we' I mean Watson and I, as Holmes finds comfort and accommodation very burdensome. Perhaps he sleeps under a nearby bridge and forces people to answer his riddles before allowing them to cross, I don't know where he goes. He only stays at the hotel on his nights with Watson, odd nights (mine are even). On my days, Holmes goes exploring in the bush alone, without a guide, and swears he runs no risk. Good for him.

I have a guide who's quite a talker; it's half natural wonder and half gossip about people I don't know and will never meet, tourists come and gone. I wonder what he'll say about me when I've departed— certainly if he ever finds out who my husband is, and his famous friend, he'll forget about me and remember them instead. My name never stands next to Sherlock Holmes, what woman's would? I will say though that my guide does remember one remarkable woman very well, insists I should look her up in England where she now lives, a mountain climber named Freda du Faur, whom he swears not only claims mountains for herself (the first to reach the top of a mountain gets to name it, and she has named at least three), but does so in a skirt. I think he might have been trying to tell me something more about Freda, when he mentioned just how staunchly unmarried she and her good friend Muriel are—Muriel lives in England now too. I wonder if my guide doesn't sense something of un-marriage about me; Watson and I are a partnership, for sure, committed and all that, but not exactly married, not when Sherlock Holmes is around.

November 11th 1921

I've decided I want to climb a mountain while I'm here, and that is what I will use my independent days to train for. Nothing too ostentatious, I won't be throwing pickaxes into rock crevices and clawing my way up anything sheer, but I would like to stand on the summit of something, and know that I've conquered it. I haven't mentioned this to the men yet, I won't bring it up until I've chosen my mountain, but I have told Watson about Freda while Holmes was lurking around us like a late-shift waiter, anxious to see our meal completed so that he could get on with his own life. From that, Watson may suspect that I'm thinking about mountain-climbing, and I'm sure Holmes already knows which peak I'll choose, though I haven't yet even heard all their names. He could make a killing as a psychic.

It is not winter on this side of the world, with every day a balmy 22-24 degrees Celsius (or 72-75 degrees Fahrenheit, which I had to learn as a child while being educated in the United States—even my teachers hardly bothered to know about Celsius, some of them perhaps assuming he was a lesser Roman emperor they'd never heard of before). If now isn't the right time to go mountain-climbing, there may never come a time. My real decision is whether or not I'll attempt to wear a skirt while I do it.

November 28th 1921

Gossip from home has arrived in our Aussie idyll. At breakfast this morning, my morning, right when Holmes was about to leave our presence with a squeeze of Watson's shoulder, Watson made a tsking sound at the paper. It was a sound that made both Holmes and I stop short, like automatons, and wait for him to tell us the scandal. We have a thousand things in common via Watson that I couldn't list if I tried, and yet somehow it's always a startling reminder when Holmes and I do something wifely in unison. I noted the oddity of it in the moment, and then did my best to banish it from my waking mind. Instead, I set myself to hoping Watson had something outrageous to share.

I'll include the clipping in question, which Watson read out over the breakfast table. The surface was nothing but detritus and coffee dregs, and Holmes was standing with his hat already on and his foot practically out the door, before this recital made him remove his hat and come back to sit again. From *The Sydney Morning Herald*'s Nov. 26th paper (it had to wander its way down to Brisbane didn't it?):

REMARKABLE LIBEL SUIT. LONDON, Nov. 24 Lord Alfred Douglas is suing the "Evening News" for libel in connection with an obituary notice published after Lord Douglas's death had been untruly reported. The news-paper's notice said: "A brilliant, unhappy career has ended. There were marked signs of degeneracy in the house of Douglas, many members of which were violently eccentric." Mr. Comyns Carr, counsel for Lord Douglas, refused to put the plaintiff in the witness box, saying that old matters would be raked up. The defence then read an extraordinary series of letters between Oscar Wilde and Lord Alfred Douglas, most of which have been published already in the course of earlier Douglas lawsuits. Lord Douglas constantly interrupted. Finally Mr. Comyns Carr asked permission to put Lord Douglas in the box. The Judge permitted this,

and Lord Douglas in evidence said he
was now ashamed of the letters he had
written. They were disgraceful.

After hearing that, I was tsking too, and Holmes looked like he had something foul he needed to hold in his mouth until he could locate an appropriate receptacle for spitting. There was a moment of silence, each of us waiting for another to break the spell, and it was Watson who eventually chipped the ice holding back a flood by wondering simply, "Why...?"

"He's a man once-burned who still plays with fire, that is why," grumbled Holmes.

I said at the same time (with less poetry but more precision, surely), "Because he's a little shit, Watson."

Holmes and I locked eyes then, and had one of our rare moments of comfortable camaraderie. Usually these moments only occur when Watson does something darling or frustrating, and we share a look like I've seen parents share over their children. However, in today's moment we were united in principle, and I must say... that flinty look of respect from Holmes was nice to receive. Perhaps Watson was even jealous, if he noticed it; Holmes usually only treats particularly wily criminals to such a grudging admiration. 'My enemy, yet my equal,' is what that look says.

Watson interrupted us. "Is it not enough that he's the one who egged Oscar Wilde into a fight with his own wretched father? He's got to deny him like the Apostle Peter over and over again?"

I told him, "He just can't resist a libel fight, darling, he's a child no matter how old he gets, and despite having a child of his own at this point. That was how Wilde got into a courtroom in the first place, wasn't it? A dirty little card left by Douglas's father calling Wilde a mean name. Infantile."

"A misspelled name at that," Watson said, nodding. "Som-do-mite."

"Posing as Som-do-mite," Holmes corrected.

"I guess he didn't like how honest that obituary was," I said, leaning closer. We all lowered our voices when this topic arose, a habit of secrecy. "Rather than correct himself for the life he has left on this earth, he'd like to argue about his unfortunate past, pick at old wounds, hold grudges he's got no business holding. What was it you told me about him and Robert Ross, dear?" I asked Watson.

"Oh, that. Holmes, you must have known more about it. You knew Robbie Ross, didn't you? Some of his friends?"

I don't know that I've recorded this before, but here I will, for posterity's sake. (*Ha, ha,* you know, in the off chance that anyone ever comes looking for the *second* woman behind the man behind the detective—stranger things have happened.) Robert Ross was such an honest man, and in my book the best friend Oscar Wilde had, not just for his support of Oscar through the trial, through prison, and after (when everyone else would have been happy to forget about him), but for what he did for Oscar's family. Poor Mrs. Wilde and the two children—no one wanted to help them much either, but Robbie did. He got them money, got Oscar's plays back on stages and making money as his executor, if not in England then at least in France. Whenever anyone published what was Oscar's, he made sure that the man's family got the profits from it. Not only that, Robbie stayed very nobly unmarried (like Freda), and mentored young men in the arts, men not unlike himself, not unlike the man Oscar Wilde turned out to be. According to Watson's gossip, Robbie is the very man who introduced Oscar to his true nature. Who knows what his honest example did to a young war poet, Wilfred Owen, who died in battle before his recognition truly found him? One of Oscar's sons died in that war too, along with my brothers, and the sons, husbands, and fathers of so many more.

I suppose my point is to say, that with all the hardship in this world, with all the losses, one ought to be a Robbie instead of a 'Bosie,' the name Douglas's mother gave him that he clearly and quite literally never outgrew. Then perhaps one wouldn't be so upset to know one's own obituary. Another young man whose talent Robbie was nurturing at the time of his death, Siegfried Sassoon (with whom that poor Wilfred Owen was quite enamored) said of Robbie's death from heart failure, "It seems reasonable to claim that this was the only occasion on which his heart failed him." Not even fifty years old when his life extinguished, and yet Robbie was able to leave a legacy so fine. Like Tom Sawyer, Robbie would have been delighted to hear what people had to say at his funeral. Douglas will probably live another twenty-odd years and still earn no better a remembrance than he has today. He got into a fight with Robbie at Oscar's funeral for Christ's sake, couldn't control himself for even one sad day. It reminds me of an old quote of Oscar's, "Some cause happiness wherever they go; others whenever they go."

Anyhow, back to today: Watson mentioned Holmes knowing Robbie because men of a certain type all did manage to know Robbie after a while, to find at least the edge of his circle. That's how Sassoon and Owen came to know him, and Holmes too would most certainly have had a friend who knew a friend who was a friend to Robbie Ross, even if they never met personally. Holmes would have the gossip, is what I mean to say.

"I knew of him," Homes confirmed. "I never had much patience for the literary set, but you see how Douglas brought them all into crosshairs with the law, and the law *is* my territory. Not just that whole upset with Wilde either—that was as much Douglas's father's doing as his, and the Marquess of Queensberry was a nasty bit of work, used to fight people in the street while brandishing that horsewhip of his. I mean long after those trials, and after Wilde died. It's as if Douglas couldn't stand the notoriety of it all; he couldn't stand being tarred with the same brush that had blackened Wilde's name, but he also didn't have any friends left in those dim parlors where he and Wilde used to go together, because he was partially to blame, wasn't he? Like his father he lashed out about it, doubled his money on a bad bet essentially, resented Robbie for being 'the good son' in a way, forgetting of course that the good son doesn't make the bad one bad, he just makes for a stark comparison. Douglas tried to get Ross prosecuted for the same crime that took down Wilde."

"He did *not*," I said, not because I doubted it was the truth, but because even knowing it I still couldn't believe it.

Holmes nodded at me somberly, just reporting the vile facts of the case as he knew them to be true. We'd nearly forgotten Watson was in the room with us at this point, wrapped up in whispers and tittle-tattle. He was watching us like he was sitting at the footlights of a play which held him rapt.

"He did, and more than once. It was a few years ago, obviously when Ross was still alive."

I glanced heavenward at that—naturally it would have been when he was still alive, thanks ever so much for assuming I might not know that, Mr. Holmes. He shook his head the slightest bit, as if to shoo a gnat; forget it, forget it, we had business to settle. Holmes went on.

"At one point a warrant was issued for Douglas's arrest. He was charged with conspiring to accuse Mr. Ross of 'an offence of a disgraceful nature.' This is a problem they were both familiar with, as there was a time, when they were both young men around Mr. Wilde, about 1893, when they'd each been involved with a boy of sixteen, the son of friends. The boy confessed it all to his parents, that he had engaged with Mr. Ross and with Lord Douglas, all while staying as a guest at Ross's house. They were both in trouble then, but after a good deal of panic, and meetings between solicitors, the parents were persuaded not to go to the police, lest their son might be seen as equally guilty. This is the system Douglas chose to toy with once more. In fact, he repeatedly went after Ross with half-truths and falsehoods."

"Grabbing a sword by the blade," Watson chimed in, with his literary way of seeing it. Holmes and I startled slightly to remember him there, and then Holmes continued.

"Douglas was brought up on libel there, but they abandoned the case, presumably when Douglas decided to let off of his offensive for a while. I'm sure the libel case he's bringing about now regarding that unfortunately early obituary will win him nothing more than a farthing in damages, but he'll shake the life out of the case anyway. He's quite a litigious man."

"Little fiend," I said.

Holmes nodded in agreement.

"You know," Watson said, his tone light again, and his voice a little louder than the snake-like hissing we'd all fallen into. "It's strange, but didn't Wilde write *The Picture of Dorian Gray* before he ever met Douglas? It's almost like he invented his own demon there, as if in writing a book with such passion as he had, he brought the story to life."

"Well, that's about the plot of the story, Watson, isn't it?" said Holmes. "No wonder it comes to your mind. The painter Basil Hallward is so enraptured with the image he makes of Dorian, he lends it demonic life."

"No, no, you misremember it, Holmes, if you ever read it that closely to begin with. In the book it is Dorian's wish that brings the painting to life after listening to the devilish suggestions of Lord Henry Wotton. Basil is the angel on his other shoulder, but in a moment of temptation Dorian makes a wish on the finished painting, that it will age so that he doesn't have to. A selfish wish, a vain wish. He suffers for it, and poor Basil suffers even more, he's murdered for it."

Holmes waved away this story, fictional and frivolous such as it was to him, though the book was real enough to be brought against Wilde as evidence in court, I do remember that. In a sense it murdered him too; Wilde certainly died much faster for having written it.

"You mean perhaps that Douglas was some sort of self-fulfilling prophecy?" I prompted Watson. "Some incubus invented by Wilde's passion, to bring him to dramatic irony and ruin?"

"Yes," Watson said, turning happily to me now, his eyes alight.

"Like the play," I told him with a smile, "very *Pygmalion*."

He started nodding fervently, and my heart burst quietly, like the tiniest firework, for I love the way he sees the world, how he can find wonder in such mundane ugliness. That's what he did in turning all of Holmes's cases into heroic stories of good triumphing over crime, is it not? That sort of thinking does make reality easier to stand; if our pain is grand, then our suffering is dignified in a way. It is our consolation farthing: in stories at least, we are the focus of cosmic and mystical powers, we are *somebody*, even if only somebody enough to be destroyed.

"I have an idea now, I must jot it down," Watson said, scrambling from his chair to find some ink and paper, leaving Holmes and I to stare across the table at each other.

Holmes said to me, "You and Watson both liked that Shaw play very much." It was another statement of fact, and yet still I answered him.

"We saw a lot of ourselves in it," I told him. We saw a lot of Holmes too, in Henry Higgins. We talked about it for days.

"You know," Holmes said, finally rising to leave, and walking towards the door as he made his parting remark. "It was *The Picture of Dorian Gray* that literally introduced Douglas to Wilde. There was a boy who loved that book, who also loved an American poet you might have heard of, Walt Whitman? If you know his work, that would tell you what kind of boy I'm speaking of."

I nodded. I knew what he meant.

"That boy saw young Douglas and gave him Wilde's book thinking he'd understand it, hoping he'd love it too. He did. It's what made Douglas so committed to Wilde at first, to meeting him and to keeping him. He was obsessed with that book." Holmes was ready to leave at that point, but stopped with his hand on the door knob, and looked towards the hallway down which Watson had disappeared. Then he turned back to me. "Tell him about that, he'll want to hear it for his story."

With that Holmes exited stage right, while Watson entered at stage left.

"Is he gone?" Watson asked. "Good. I've decided to write a short fiction story, but I don't want him to know about it yet."

Instead of telling Watson that he knew already, I told him my own open secret.

I said, "Darling, I'm going to climb a mountain. I won't tell if you won't!"

October 11th 1921

The mountain I've chosen near here is called Mermaid Mountain, more on that later. Watson has finished his story and asked me to type it up for him. I'll include a carbon copy here with my own papers, it's darling:

THE NIGHTMARE PYGMALION

Mr. Henry Hawkins arrives in his attic office exactly on time this morning, which is not his usual habit. Mr. Hawkins tends to linger at breakfast, even after his wife and his sons have moved on from the table to start their own days. He'll often ask for second helpings, open a book to read as if every morning could be a Sunday morning, for he knows that once he quits the table and ascends to the top of his home, he will have to stay there until he has completed either eight pages of something (writing or editing) or eight hours of time has passed. His lunches will be brought to him, because if he leaves this dreary office for even a moment he does not want to return, and if he interrupts his eight hours in the middle, he still has to complete them late into the night, which his wife and housekeeper do not appreciate. There were one or two golden days when this system was first put in place—a system to treat his writing work the same as any other man's work, who must go to his office in the city each day—when Mr. Hawkins finished quickly

14

and efficiently, and freed himself for the rest of the day. Most of the time, however, he must wage gruelling battle with his own procrastination. Mr. Hawkins can be his own worst enemy.

This morning, thankfully, is different. It is a rare and special morning, where Mr. Hawkins knows he is on the cusp of finishing a project, and not just any project—not an article or a piece of someone else's editing that he's doing for pay—this is his own dear novel. The draft is nearly complete, and he has been editing his own pages for the past week, hoping that by the time the end arrived, which is today, he would know how to complete it.

In this story, a young boy actor is found to be so extraordinary by both a playwright and a theater owner that he becomes monstrous in his ability to play them against each other. It is, or so Mr. Hawkins hopes, a battle for the boy's soul between the choices of love and money. Art versus commerce! The war is ugly, but the story becomes truly thrilling when the boy himself decides to take the ultimate revenge on his tormentors. Terrified that when he's too old for the most sensational roles he won't matter enough to have any choice at all, and worried that his new-found power will soon be gone like fog under the rising sun, he gets a play written just for him put on stage, and promoted for the largest audience possible. At the story's climax, when his character is meant to plunge a dagger into his heart, the boy allows life to imitate art: he uses a real dagger instead of a prop dagger, and brings fiction horribly to life.

Mr. Hawkins has written up to this point in the story. This could be an ending unto itself, but he wants the story to live longer, so that he can dwell more within it. Of course, he can always use the money for a higher word count, but for his own choice when it comes to love or money, today it appears he can have both; he doesn't want to return downstairs to his squalling sons and tired wife. He wants to remain aloft from them here, where he can bring this remarkable boy back to life. He has every incentive to push on.

When Mr. Hawkins sets down his editing pen today, he does not turn to his typewriter, but instead writes by hand, because he is still faster with a pen than on that contraption he considers to be a glorified adding machine. Without a single drop of coffee this morning, his hand flies and his thoughts are electric. The zeal of creation is upon him, and he's missed it so very much lately.

The boy will die on that stage, but he will not stay dead. His tormented spirit will linger in the eaves and wings of the theater, will grow with malevolent power enough to bring dramatic justice to the men who had been happy to pull his life apart for their own self-interests. When the theater owner finds a fresh, young, hopeful girl, and convinces her to sing dirty songs with her skirt hiked up, the Spirit will strangle her voice until she leaves the theater mute, but unsullied. When the playwright finds a new young man to fill the parts the dead boy has left empty, and beats him when he doesn't perform them just the same way, the spirit embodies the boy with strength enough to fight back, beating the playwright to death backstage. That young man goes to prison while the spirit returns to his roost in the playhouse, but so be it. The Spirit's sense of injustice does not lead him to right wrongs necessarily, but to take revenge, regardless of the tiny lives that are snuffed out in service of the greater picture.

Mr. Hawkins forgets the hours entirely, writing until his hand cramps, and then beating the table with furious vehemence to loosen up his fist. He cannot stop, and will not stop until he finds the end.

The Spirit, emboldened by its ability to possess a body, seeks the strength to steal one. To take control of a body over from its natural owner, so that the Spirit can leave the playhouse again. Not only will the Spirit be able to walk the earth once more, if it can learn to move from body to body, it can be young and alive always, and live forever.

The story comes to its climax when Mr. Hawkins writes the Spirit into another body, a working-class youth who is in the theater apprenticing with the set builder. This boy is Italian; swarthy, golden, and strong, with thick black hair and luscious lips. The Spirit stretches his arms out inside this body, as one might slide into a rich, luxurious coat, and when he can move the fingers, he brings them to the body's mouth. They smell of wood. The nails are strong and blunt. The Spirit both touches the lips and kisses the fingers, two acts in one movement. He can feel the Italian boy's spirit as if it is close behind him, but it has no real strength to force him out.

"Don't worry, young man," he says with the lips. "This won't last forever." *Only I shall last forever*, the Spirit thinks, and with that, he walks out of the playhouse vowing to never return.

Mr. Hawkins sits back when he strikes the last period on this page, and only then realizes how much his hand hurts. He cradles it, massages and stretches it, terribly sorry he had to use it so poorly, but in the end he knows this pain was worth it. His hand will mend, but this story... this story could only have happened in a trance, and this story will last longer than mortal flesh.

Mr. Hawkins smiles to himself; he's swallowed up his own fiction, thinking like that, of immortality. He picks up his pen one last time, to finish the story by signing his name to the pages—of course this is not the final draft, it will have to be typed up tomorrow, but it feels like the proper completion to this brief fever of conception. He will sign it like a contract, wishing in spite of the satisfaction its completion gives him, that the mad energy of this story would never end, that it could become real, and save him from the inevitable monotony that his ceaseless working days will bring.

Oh well, Mr. Hawkins thinks, flourishing his name and dropping his pen once more. He goes downstairs, and to bed.

*

The following days are indeed dull for Mr. Hawkins. He puts his story to rest knowing that he needs some distance before he can fully edit it for submission, and in the meantime he must answer to his wife as to what he was banging around about upstairs. His desk-pounding woke their youngest child from his nap, and moreover he must treat his battered hand quite gingerly as he cleans up some of his necessary chores—addressing magazine heads, paying bills, meeting his editing obligations, and consoling himself for the loss of his too-temporary thrill. It is no wonder to Mr. Hawkins why Dr. Jekyll couldn't keep his hands off the potion that gave him the freedom to be Edward Hyde; Mr. Hawkins can hardly keep his hands off the gin in his desk drawer. For the next week, following the completion of his story, he takes sips of it between breakfast and lunch, just to get a little thrill for his work. He hopes his wife doesn't smell it on his breath.

He hopes the maid doesn't note the descending level when she comes in to dust.

Luckily for Mr. Hawkins, there's a distraction in his house: a project of his wife's friends, a boy stranded in England alone while his school is on holiday and his parents are in transition, moving from Canada to England. He has nowhere to stay, and someone had the idea that he might be of decent use in the Hawkins house—not necessarily to make him work for his supper, mind, but to apprentice him with a working man of letters. Why, not only would it help Mr. Hawkins free up time for his family, but the young man might be greatly improved to learn of real work before he graduates, so it doesn't shock his system. Young men can come out of university with too much idealism sometimes, and it makes the transition to the real world quite difficult. Mr. Hawkins knows that feeling all too well, and that sympathy above anything else convinces him to take on a ward for a few months. Letters are exchanged with the young man's family, and their friends stake their confidence in the Hawkins household as a suitable place where the young sir will come to no nasty influence. If only they knew. But Mr. Hawkins only tells his truths in his fictions, for if one tells the truth, one is sure, sooner or later...

The young man is called Ariel Xavier Edwards (his parents are lovers of Shakespeare, thus his spritely name), and he is Canadian, though he and his family are moving to England for the indefinite future. Mr. Hawkins finds that charming right away, for he is Irish, and though he trained himself to hide his accent while he was at university, he's often reminded that he doesn't fully belong here. Certainly he drinks with more natural aptitude than the English, not that they would credit him for that if they knew how much gin he's been putting away before the noon hour.

It's agreed the boy will stay at the Hawkins house. They send a car to fetch him from the train station, and he arrives at the house fresh-faced and cheery, like someone who was not raised in London gloom. Light brown hair, and an easy smile, with lashes that flutter over his eyes like the wings of gentle moths. Master Ariel had a sunny childhood, and it shows on him. He greets the children first, then kisses the hand of Mrs. Hawkins, and then comes to Mr. Hawkins at last to shake his hand.

"Thank you for sparing the time for me, sir, I know you are a busy man."

Mr. Hawkins had not been busy enough before Master Ariel's arrival. A change is indeed as good as a rest; with someone to dictate to, with another pair of eyes for work that has become meaningless with scrutiny, suddenly Mr. Hawkins doesn't have enough work and begins to take on more. His wife is so pleased that she finds the time to bake a cake for his upcoming birthday, his 32nd, and makes sure Master Ariel is included, since he's been such a cleansing zephyr through this house. Work is going out and money is coming in with better speed and accounting, and her husband no longer trudges up to his office, nor does he come slumping back down, but instead he leaves and returns with pep in his step. He just needed a second wind perhaps, after settling down into married life. He needed someone young around, someone to talk to who wasn't a woman or a baby, but instead a disciple. She tells him this, and Mr. Hawkins wonders if she isn't right: perhaps this was what he was missing, and it's a role his own sons will fill someday when they are older and need to learn the ways of the world. Master

Ariel has reminded him that there is more in life to look forward to other than the slow and steady drudgery of responsibility. Bless him.

The day of Mr. Hawkins's birthday brings a wonderful turning point, when all of his correspondence is up-to-date, and he has a brisk schedule laid out for deadlines and work minimums on a calendar of Master Ariel's making. At last he feels he is ahead of his work and not behind the Sisyphean boulder of it. Therefore it is with relief and satisfaction that he turns to the drawer with his small novel, as yet untitled, about the boy who ascends to a vengeful spirit. He will want Master Ariel to read it first, before he sees it again himself, just to see if it has even half the effect on the page as the idea of it holds within his own mind.

As they descend downstairs for the birthday dinner and festivities, Mr. Hawkins asks the favor.

"Master Ariel, would you be so kind as to join me for a drink once the children are in bed? I have an extra bit of work, more a labor of love than anything that is yet under contract, but... I would like for you to read it and give me your thoughts. Not an edit, you understand, but your opinion on its subject matter and quality."

"Certainly, Mr. Hawkins," he said, grasping Mr. Hawkins on the shoulder while they are still unseen on the stairs. "I'm honored you would put such value in my judgement." He's so earnest in his gratitude that Mr. Hawkins feels strange, almost as if he'd missed a step going down, though he certainly did not. All the same, it feels as if the bottom has dropped out from under him, and he doesn't quite know where he stands as Master Ariel continues past him.

The children make a mess of their small pieces of cake, so after a round of 'Happy Birthday' and some pulled crackers, it's a rather short little party. The women go to clean up the children, and the men retire for a drink. This will not be a drink of drawer gin in a windowless attic, however. They go to the sitting room, and Mr. Hawkins pours some brandy. He has fetched the manuscript down from the rafters, and watches surreptitiously as the boy strokes his finger down each page, pointing over each line as he reads it. He accepts his glass of brandy without looking up, sipping distractedly from one hand, and turning over pages with the other.

When he gets to the handwritten portion, Master Ariel begins to squint, and Mr. Hawkins moves a lamp closer to his side. His face changes as he comprehends the story: first he was expectant, then seemingly concerned, and now his face is tensed as if he might scream at any moment. Mr. Hawkins worries that his beloved story isn't any good, or that it is good but too objectionably grotesque for Master Ariel to stomach. When Master Ariel's finger finally passes over the signature at the end, he looks up slightly, as if searching himself for something to say.

"I am prepared for your true opinion, and will not hold it against you," Mr. Hawkins says. If it's a bad review, that is his tragedy and not the boy's; he does want to make that clear.

Master Ariel's face twitches with what appears to be a smile, before he cocks his head suddenly to look at Mr. Hawkins. Then he smiles, a fast and wicked smile more worldly than one would expect from such a young and sheltered boy, and quite different from the smiles Mr. Hawkins has seen from him before.

"It's quite inventive," he says before adding a delayed, "sir." His eyes perk, as if he's pleased he remembered to be polite. "It really comes alive."

Mr. Hawkins feels a great plunge of relief, as intense as if he'd finished his drink in one gulp.

"Do you really think so? Is it that powerful? Certainly I felt it was some of my best work when I finished it, but I've been let down before in the light of day, I've found that my ambition was greater than my ability, and…"

Mr. Hawkins is silenced and surprised by the touch of Master Ariel's fingers on his lips. That is rather forward of a boy who's been nothing but deferential and respectful for his entire tenure in this house, as a schoolboy to a master. Now he stands before Mr. Hawkins as bold as brass, his eyes intense and knowing, shushing him.

"I am curious, what inspired you to write this story?"

"I… I suppose…" Mr. Hawkins begins with a stammer.

"Don't you know?" Master Ariel asks.

When Mr. Hawkins has no answer, for he feels mesmerized by Master Ariel's stare, the boy dismisses him.

"When you figure it out, let me know," Master Ariel says, before taking his glass of brandy with him to bed, and leaving the story behind.

It was a strange night, and the week that follows is stranger every day. The first day is Sunday, and instead of accompanying the family on their walk through the park, instead of dressing and amusing himself with the children and taking the air with them, Master Ariel said he could not, that he was sick. Did he need tending? No. Was he feverish? No. Was he truly sick? He didn't look sick, but he assured them that he was, and so they let him be.

By Monday, when it comes time to resume work, Master Ariel still declines. Mrs. Hawkins finds this very concerning, says if it happens again she might have to write to Master Ariel's mother, that as a woman she knows this behavior would concern her if it were one of her sons. Mr. Hawkins promises her that if it happens again, he will speak to the young man about it, find out what the trouble is, though he already suspects... It was something to do with his story, wasn't it? Or perhaps the alcohol, does Master Ariel have a weakness for it that no one was aware of? Mr. Hawkins resolves he will get to the bottom of it before his wife writes any letters. On Tuesday he stops by Master Ariel's room after breakfast, finds his tray of food savaged and waiting to be retrieved. Mr. Hawkins has a plan to keep his house peaceful—he will check on Master Ariel, leave him some work he can do alone and at his leisure, and surely that will be agreeable to everyone?

On Tuesday evening, Mr. Hawkins comes to find the pages he left have been marked, not with editing notes, but with nonsense. There are scribbles, dark gashes from the pencil, so much that the work underneath is nearly indecipherable in some places. It gets worse until there is a tear in one page, evidence of the pencil snapping, and then the rest of the pages are untouched. Mr. Hawkins is incensed, ready to be either offended or profoundly scared, for this is either Master Ariel taking some childish revenge on the man so kind as to host him, or Master Ariel has had some sort of secret stroke, and knows not how to ask for the help he needs very badly and very quickly.

Mr. Hawkins gets his keys and barges into the room to confront the boy, but the room is empty. When he asks the maid, she only knows that he was there to accept breakfast, and she has not yet brought dinner. They search the house from top to bottom together, but the boy is nowhere to be found. Mr. Hawkins tells the maid to leave it to him. Will he have to bring in the police? How to explain this missing man? He's young but he's not a child, he's inexperienced but not truly their ward, he's a university man! Mr. Hawkins searches the darkening street and the alleys around his home first, hoping to find some clue before he has to involve his wife and come to some decision, and he believes he is in luck when he sees a figure staggering down the lane whose build he recognizes. There's the boy! Is he sick, injured, robbed, confused? What has happened to him?

Mr. Hawkins runs to him, only to catch him before he over-balances and begins to fall. Mr. Hawkins manages to absorb his momentum, turning them both into a dance-hall twirl to keep them standing.

It turns out, Master Ariel is not weaving because he is sick, he's like this because he is drunk, Mr. Hawkins smells it on him as soon as he grabs hold of the boy. What has happened to the boy, how did he come to this wretchedness so suddenly?

Mr. Hawkins does not scold him in the street. He brings the boy inside, sloppy and hanging on his shoulders like a limp marionette. He does his best to get him up to the attic before anyone can emerge to question this commotion. He puts the boy in his office chair, and slaps him to get his focus. Master Ariel startles to feel it, but then flexes his jaw and smiles, a grin as wide as the Cheshire cat.

"What the devil has gotten into you, Master Ariel?" Mr. Hawkins asks.

"That is not my name," he says. "Not Devil, not Ariel."

"Where have you been? You're babbling drunk, you're disgraceful!"

"I found... friends," Master Ariel says, his head rolling dramatically around on his shoulders. With his eyes adjusting to the light, Mr. Hawkins notices that Master Ariel's shirt is halfway open under his jacket, his shoes and trousers are splashed with muck up to the knees, and there is blood on his knuckles, as if he's been fighting.

"Do you hit your friends?" Mr. Hawkins asks, picking up his hand to showcase the evidence. Master Ariel clutches his fingers, and brings them to his jaw, where there is a bruise blooming under the shadow of his chin.

"They hit me, here, for I had gambled with them and won. They did not want me to win, so they hit me. But look, I hit them harder; look at what I have."

Master Ariel pulls money out of his pockets, badly crumpled paper, and coins. The coins bounce and roll, making a racket. Mr. Hawkins grabs the boy's hands again.

"Gambling and drinking. What else have you done?"

"A woman," he says. "She gave me drinks, and she tried to consume me." He brings his hands, and Mr. Hawkins's hands, together to the joint where his manhood lies. "I did not let her. I hit her too."

Drinking, gambling, and whoring. How sheltered must this boy have been to have broken free so wildly? Why did it have to be under his watch, why not at school with boys his own age? This would be a scandal for everyone involved if it were ever to get out, even in rumor. Mr. Hawkins will have to lock this boy in his attic until he can be rid of him.

He shakes off Master Ariel's grip and goes about readying the room. He gathers all of his papers and locks them inside the desk. He will take the candle with him so there's no risk of fire. He will take his clock and his pictures, in case Master Ariel becomes destructive, or more fearful yet, self-destructive. Master Ariel watches him placidly all the while. He appears to be sobering.

When Mr. Hawkins has set his valuables outside the door, he tells the boy, "You should sleep. There is a cot in the corner I use for napping, you will sleep there. I'll bring you your breakfast in the morning and we will talk, like men. If you're going to act like this you can stop that doe-eyed nonsense you came here with, acting so innocent when you clearly knew enough to go out carousing."

"Ca-rous-ing," he says, flexing his jaw again, since it must still hurt. Mr. Hawkins goes to leave in a hurry, remembering how he slapped the boy to get his attention before knowing that he'd been out brawling. Now he is concerned that Master Ariel might strike him back, and he doesn't want that at all.

"Goodnight," he says, turning for the door, when suddenly there's a grip on his shirt from behind, a strong grip.

"What is my name?"

Mr. Hawkins assumes this is more drunk-talk, some kind of mangled pride trying to come to the surface, some kind of vanity. Mr. Hawkins puts his weight into escaping the boy's grip, feels his shirt coming untucked, but rushes from the room unconcerned about the cloth being torn. He locks the door behind him.

Master Ariel slams against it, and pounds the door once when he finds it fastened against him.

"You owe me my name," he says, but then goes to the other end of the room by the sound of his dragging feet.

Hopefully he will pass out and wake up with some sense, Mr. Hawkins wishes, before he realizes that he left the candle in there. He won't risk going back in now. He dreams that night of infernos, but wakes up safely.

Mr. Hawkins only goes to breakfast to tell the family Master Ariel has been recovered, may need a doctor, and is in the attic for now, but please don't worry. "I will do the worrying for the family. This is my responsibility."

It is his responsibility, and his burden. Mr. Hawkins brings a tray of food upstairs, only to find Master Ariel awake, having tossed around his precious books. It looks as if he's pulled them all off the shelf looking for some secret escape hatch, haphazardly, desperately. Most of them are flung on the ground, and yet Master Ariel sits on the bed with a mosaic of some, each book laid open and fit onto the mattress like pieces of a puzzle. He is frowning, not reading any specific one, but looking between each of them as if they were books of research and not works of fiction.

"My God," Mr. Hawkins hisses when he comes in. He sets the tray down, closes the door, and then starts picking up his books from the floor. "You horrible brat, what have you done?"

"I can read, but I cannot write, isn't that curious? I suppose I'll want to learn."

He's either still drunk or gone purely mad, Mr. Hawkins surmises.

"Of course you can write, you were writing for me last week."

"Master Ariel can write. I wonder, since he knows how to write, if I might simply need practice with the fingers."

He starts trying to steeple his fingers together, but keeps missing, and unevenly clasping them together instead.

"That is it. Will you get me some writing implements out of your desk? You locked it, you know, which seems very unkind."

"Mrs. Hawkins is about to write to your mother, would you like me to tell her all that you've been doing?"

"I have no mother," says the boy, with contempt of the level one might have when talking to an arrogant simpleton. "I was born of your mind, like Athena from

Zeus." He holds up a book on mythology as if it is fact. Maybe he consumed more substances than alcohol?

"Master Ariel..." Mr. Hawkins begins, but he is interrupted.

"I am not he, I am the Spirit. I would like a better name, and if you don't give me one, I will choose my own. Ariel doesn't like me, but he can't move me from his vessel. I am stronger than him. I will learn to use his fingers."

"What are you on about?" Mr. Hawkins says, still preoccupied with his books but finally starting to feel the tendrils of dread in his heart. Master Ariel has been very unlike himself lately. Is he truly mad, and if so, what brought it on so quickly?

The boy gets up from the bed, and starts collecting together the books he was looking at, copying Mr. Hawkins, and bringing the tomes to him.

"I have come out of the rafters, Father," he says, handing over the books in deference. "What is my name?"

"Don't call me that," said Mr. Hawkins. "You're not one of my sons, and you presume too much if you think that affection extends to you."

"They are not your sons, I am your son. I am your Adam."

"You are Mr. Edwards, and I have no responsibility towards..."

The boy silences Mr. Hawkins by grabbing his throat with a severe grip. His eyes are hideously calm.

"The previous inhabitant of this body is under my power. You, at this moment, are under my power. You will not repeat the mistakes of the men in your own story, surely. You must know better than that."

Now a cold fear grips Mr. Hawkins even more forcefully than Master Ariel's hand. Could this be the Spirit of the boy from his story? How? More importantly, why? Did his wish in wanting his story to be real come so terribly true? If so, then of all the wishes in all his life, why was this the one that was granted? He's wished for more wealth, better luck, better looks, but this one idle fancy is the one that manifests? To ruin an innocent boy, and soon enough Mr. Hawkins's own reputation, possibly his whole life?

For all his indignation, however, Mr. Hawkins knows instinctually why. He has indeed wished for things before, but never with such longing and fervor as he had the night of that story. In that moment he wanted nothing more than an upset to his boring, respectable life. He thought Master Ariel would become that for him, and in an unexpected way, he was right.

As if this new entity can read his mind, he says, "You like this body too much. He knew it, though he suspected that you did not, not really. When he touched your shoulder, you shied from him. He was prepared to thank you very much for sharing my story with him, he was going to… what is his idea? Seduce you. That will never happen now. Now you must seduce me, you must treasure me, you must bring me everything I demand and more, do you understand?"

At that, this creature releases Mr. Hawkins and expects him to speak. Instead, Mr. Hawkins brings his infernal story out of the desk, finds the candle and match he left behind the night before, and lights the wick. This monstrous abomination only watches him, as placid as a crocodile, and doesn't move to stop his hand.

"Do you understand?" Mr. Hawkins taunts back. "This story isn't so valuable to me that I won't destroy it to destroy you." He starts setting fire to the pages, thinking this is a great and noble sacrifice he's making—destroying his own beloved art for the good of young Master Ariel—but Ariel's face only smirks at him, under the Spirit's control.

"I have left those pages," it explains to Mr. Hawkins, watching the only evidence of this ghastly transfer of power, this demonic contract, go up in smoke. "To get rid of me, you might try killing this body, but you won't harm this body you lust after so much, or the prisoner I hold within it. In fact, even if you did, I might take control of your body instead. I would certainly try."

Mr. Hawkins knows he will not chance that, and is even more sure that it would take a great deal more horror to force him to murder anyone, he's too much the coward. Perhaps this Spirit can be reasoned with, perhaps it can be harnessed? Perhaps, since it seems so desperate to learn, it can be taught responsibly.

"I think... you will find that the name you've borrowed already suits you," Mr. Hawkins says slowly. He moves so that Master Ariel's body can take a seat at the desk. "I will bring you the play it is from tonight. You can read, you said? Can you spell?"

"S-P-E-L-L," responds the Spirit Ariel. "I could recreate your entire story, my story. I have it remembered, even its mistakes."

"Well... I suppose you could do that with a typewriter then," Mr. Hawkins says, removing the machine's cover and rolling a sheet of paper through it. "You'll find it easier than writing by hand. You'll resume your apprenticeship, Master Ariel, until you have mastered writing?"

"What happens next?" the Spirit asks.

Mr. Hawkins does not know, but he wishes—perhaps as recklessly as he did over his initial story—that this mix of man and sprite would remain with him, devoted to his maker the way even the most faithful son cannot be. He touches Ariel's hair, the curve of one curl, and knows for sure in this moment that he may do so without fear of revulsion or retaliation. Master Ariel, despite what this creature says, may have ultimately rebelled at his touch, but the Spirit Ariel wants its maker's devotion, needs it.

Very well; Mr. Hawkins desires the same devotion in return.

Honestly: that I chose Mermaid Mountain while Watson chose Shakespeare's Ariel is pretty preternatural don't you think? We've got a ghostly link in that Hans Christian Andersen story, don't we? Perhaps I read too much into these sorts of things, but it seems clever now that it's occurred to me, seems at least fitting and neat.

I've given Watson my notes on his story. We won't remain in Australia through the winter—despite how comfortable the weather is here versus England, we will have to sail back home before the ice becomes too dangerous. I have a mountain to climb, and now even on my days with Watson, I take him out walking with me, on familiar paths just to maintain my progress and increase my stamina. Perhaps he will want to climb a mountain of his own before we leave. Perhaps he will join me!

October 28th 1921

Our departure is now set for the second week of November. Apparently whatever business Holmes needed to attend to here is sorted, and there's no reason to stay except to find the most comfortable passage and book our tickets. I shall attempt my climb next week.

November 4th 1921

Congratulate me, diary, for I have not perished! Watson was not so fortunate. He is not dead, but he is injured, and will have to use our long journey home to convalesce. My guide drove us all, including Holmes, to the town of Mt. Crosby, and arranged to shuffle cars with another fellow, so that at the end of an 18-kilometer hike (about 11 of the king's miles), a car would drive us back around the mountain to where we left the first one, and then all would be on our way back home. Unfortunately, Watson fell and twisted his ankle within the first three miles, and though I was ready to abandon my mountain, every man around me assured me the injury was mild. The guide said he would help Watson back down and get him to a local doctor he knew, and he told Holmes and me that the trail was marked, that we already had our maps, and that he would meet us with Watson on the other side if I wanted to continue. Well... I did! Although I wasn't exactly pleased that I found myself unexpectedly on a private walk through the woods with Sherlock Holmes.

We said nothing for miles. About halfway up the mountain we were treated to a great view of Lake Manchester and the surrounding hills. This trail is supposed to take about five hours to complete, it took us six what with Watson's mishap, and with stopping so I could catch my breath and gaze at the lake. Holmes pointed out a few curiosities along the way, literally pointed without speaking, and only once verbally warned me to watch out for a snake. That is what prompted our sole bit of conversation.

"Watson finished his story," he stated. "Have you read it?"

"I have," I responded. I didn't ask if he'd read it. He might know all about it even if Watson is still keeping it a secret from him.

"What did you think of it?"

Again, there's no knowing if Holmes has read it or not. I answered him anyway.

"I thought it was quite good. I could see elements of Dorian Gray in there, but also of Frankenstein's monster, and of Dr. Jekyll and Mr. Hyde most of all—he's always liked that one particularly."

"That he has," Holmes said.

I happen to know that my dear Watson got Holmes to read the Stevenson book once, and that Holmes threw the copy at his head in thanks; Holmes doesn't appreciate moralizing when it comes to him instead of from him, but there's never a time to point out all I know about their shared past. I have the future of Watson, and that is enough.

We came then to a particularly awkward boulder, and had to stop talking to climb up and over it. I could tell Holmes was waiting to see if I'd need his help to get over the rock without falling, but he would not offer it to me until I couldn't refuse, and before that moment I managed it on my own with a lot of huffing and puffing. I don't know how Freda du Faur does this sort of stuff in a skirt; I was having trouble in the most sensible trousers I could find. After I caught my breath back, Holmes talked on.

"Do you think he'll ever publish this story?"

"Not while he's alive, with its subject matter, but he might let me do it, after he's gone. And of course, if he were worried about it being attached to his name, and your legacy, we could always put it under my maiden name, since it's so unknown."

Holmes nodded with a slight smile, but did not answer. I suppose he'll let Watson and I sort that out, as we didn't speak of it, or of anything else, for the rest of the journey.

It did cause me to think though, on the descent, that if Oscar Wilde created his own monster with Dorian Gray, then what did Watson make when he took Sherlock Holmes and made him fiction? There was an exchange I found, in flipping through the copy of *The Picture of Dorian Gray* that Watson procured here for aid in writing his story, that I remembered on the trail and am still pondering now:

"You are glad you have met me, Mr. Gray," said Lord Henry, looking at him.

"Yes, I am glad now. I wonder shall I always be glad?"

A Boston Marriage

January 2nd 1924

I am so sick of this cold. I keep thinking longingly of Australia, the summer they're having down under while the rest of us in this hemisphere are freezing our bits and tips off. If only the journey wasn't so tedious, I'd hop down there every winter and back here for a delightful spring and English summer, but that is not the life I am currently tolerating.

However, on remembering that one glorious trip we took to Queensland in '21, something has been percolating in the teapot on the back burner of my mind. As I long to go hiking again in fresh mountain air, I remember Freda du Faur and her secret love, and in contemplating the romance of it all, it suddenly occurred to me... I have known a woman like her all my life.

My cousin, Miss Emelda Clara, or as I've always known her, Mellie. She was a breath of sorority in a childhood full of brothers, five years younger than me and terribly sweet and pretty to me every time we met. She was an only child, and in meeting my team of brothers knew she did not want one of those icky things, and fixated ever so flatteringly upon me. I was so worldly going to school in America, I was so mouthy in a way she would never dare, I never blushed no matter what the boys said around me (the things girls talk about in boarding schools would have melted them with shame to hear; I was immune to boyish lewdness), and I loved her too. I treated her like a living doll, braiding her hair and spoiling her with treats and trinkets, while she remembered me with something crocheted every Christmas. Sweet girl, but the reason I've been thinking of her lately is because of the stories I've heard about the woman she's become.

Mellie has never married. She should be about forty-five or forty-six years old now, and instead of a husband, she has taken on a roommate of sorts, last I heard, an independent woman and heiress who minds her family's holdings. This person apparently welcomes Mellie as a companion, to avoid the misery of an empty house, as well as enjoy the comfort of a housekeeper. Basically, Mellie has gotten all the duties and comforts of being a wife without the marriage. Recently it has dawned on me: is Mellie in a different sort of marriage? A marriage that, in one very key way, is as unusual as my own?

My last communication with Mellie (after the flood of reconnection following the war) was when reports of a nasty storm hitting the south coast prompted me to write to her in Brighton, and ask how well they fared, whether the storm had impacted them at all. That was nearly five years ago, so I think it's time for another hello, don't you? Here's the letter I posted today.

> *Hello my Mellie,*
>
> *Too much time has passed since last I heard about you. Is life treating you well? Mr. Watson and I are doing fine, doing wonderfully if I really think about it: we're in good health and better spirits and are occupied by pleasant domestic distractions like reorganizing the library (me) and penning papers for publication (Watson). Sometimes I think I'm*

bored, but am able to quickly remind myself that every exciting time in my life was excruciating, and then I usually just take a nap so that my dreams might entertain me.

How are you? How blissful is your domesticity and how domestic your bliss? I do hope that you are as bored with contentment as I am, and that we can schedule a visit soon, perhaps some time this year? You must see my face again before it is wizened beyond recognition, and I must see you so I can spiritually siphon some of your youth away. Oops! Disregard that last part, I mean only to enjoy the pleasure of your company—my place or yours, which is more agreeable to you? I won't take 'no' for an answer.

My best to George, your helpers, your creatures, and all the ships at sea.

Sincerely your
Cozante

'Cozante' is the name she invented for me as a child, both 'cousin' and 'auntie' and a bit of rudimentary spelling thrown in. It would have made a great code name had I been spy material during the war, but alas, just a pair of helping hands that liked to organize. Surely not many people call Emelda by Mellie these days, but she is always Mellie to me, just as I am forever her Cozante.

George, of course, is her dear friend and companion Georgina Mae Addington, who often tells people they "Mae" call her George. The name George does suit her better, as well as her tailor-made suits for a woman's frame. This is why I wonder, you see, not about George (very few people wonder about George), but about my Mellie. Have I missed truly seeing her this whole time?

January 20th 1924
I received my reply from Mellie today, and boy has it answered a couple of questions and raised a few more. Here's the transcript:

Darling Cozante!

You would have the presentiment to know you'd be wanted just when there is an occasion to summon you—the weekend after St. Valentine's Day, could you come? George is throwing us a party for a few reasons, not least of which is the surprise that I am being adopted. We've been living in what George calls a 'Boston marriage,' two independent women making a house together, but this is a step beyond.

It may sound strange, I know, but with my own mother and father dead and beyond offending, and the laws being what they are, if George wants to grant me all the rights of family over her own terrible relatives, that is what her barrister says must be done. G's sister married a particularly vile specimen who keeps having children in the hopes of a son to take away George's inheritance someday—he keeps getting daughters like Henry VIII and treats them like disappointments. If those girls have any of the same pluck that George has they'll make him sorry for that in due time.

Anyway, must save some gossip for when we meet, if you can come? Mr. Watson is of course welcome as well, and as treasured family members you can stay in the house with us, just let me know as quickly as possible so I can air the room and lay down the welcoming carpet. The icky family will be there too, but mostly for entertainment purposes and George's joy in conquering men at their own silly games.

Please come and show how superior my side of the family is.
Your Mellie

Well that's Valentine's weekend sorted, isn't it? Watson and I shall go, of course, and bring flowers, and don't think I didn't notice the coincidence that Mellie's new family was coming together under the banner of St. Valentine—a happy coincidence I'm sure.

February 12th 1924

Well, the journey to Mellie's was a real test of marital integrity for Watson and me. You know that icy silence that sits between husband and wife as you both work very hard not to snap at one another? It was there, and we both knew it all the while, but held our tongues and are back in love again now that we've been able to get away from each other for five consecutive minutes. All those conflicting instructions and 'I told you so's left unsaid are forgotten and all is forgiven. We live to stay wed another day.

The party won't be until Friday, the 15th, so we have a little time to rest and help out before the hullabaloo commences. After a change of clothes and splash of water to the face, we were greeted by our hosts, and I went straight to Mellie like a shot. She's so grown! She's over forty and I just can't believe it. The last time I saw her, it was before she met George, still timid and girlish in many ways, the dutiful old maid everyone expected her to be, and then today I laid my eyes on her again, and found a true vision. There she was, standing with one hand on her hip, and the other pointing out features of the room to be decorated like she was a professional hired for the task. When she spotted me, however, my little doll shone through again.

"Cozante, I've missed you!" she proclaimed, throwing open her arms. I nearly started crying as I hugged her, hadn't realized just how badly I'd been missing her until I saw her again, but I soldiered through it and squeezed her with vigor.

"Look at you!" I said. "You look so happy, your skin is pink with it like a woman half your age."

Separating, we held onto each other's elbows and feasted our eyes. Many a mother and daughter pair would be jealous of a pure love like that which we have. We were lost in a waterfall of wonder until Watson cleared his throat, waking us from our enchantment. That is when I first set eyes on George.

Without knowing that George was Georgina, I would have assumed this was a man I was speaking to, perhaps someone in charge of building or delivering something for the party. With a heft of body that suggested a former athlete and the stance of someone who did not plait their legs together when sitting, it was only slowly over the rest of the afternoon that I had time to notice: the bulge of the chest as if there were indeed smothered bosoms under there, and the little movements many of us girls have of touching up our hair just at the ear, just with the lightest nudge of our ring fingers. Those hints, coupled with her rather clear, high voice, were all that reminded one that George was not the man of the house, but its mistress.

"If I may so call you Cozante as well," George said, taking my hand like a gentleman. "We are soon to be family after all, and I know you by no other name from all of Em's stories."

"That is fine," I said, "if I may call you by George?"

"Please do," George said, with a slight bow, releasing back my hand. "Those who call me Georgina Mae may find themselves entirely ignored." George stepped back and took Watson and myself in as a pair, and found us satisfactory. "Are the Watsons hungry at all?"

We were, and lunch was had in a sunny room far from the kitchen, as that room was being cleaned and organized for the catering job to come. The sunlight kept us from being too cold as we ate sandwiches and sipped tea, and the view, though still a bit bleak during February, was nevertheless nice enough that I understood why this place was once so popular before the war as a sea-bathing retreat spot, and why it was then used during and after the war for convalescing soldiers. Mellie, it turned out, loved to swim.

"If you say I don't look my age," she told me as our meal wound down, "I believe it has to do with swimming. The exercise, the fresh air, the salt scrub against my skin, it keeps me younger than I ought to be."

"Some people have gone in for *drinking* the seawater," George said, leaning forward for a matchbox to light a post-lunch cigarette. "Drives folks mad who were ever shipwrecked, but somehow these landed types believe it will do them some good."

"I'm glad you know that it won't," Watson said, forever a doctor. "Too much salt and it dehydrates the rest of the body just to produce urine, and after a sustained overdose of salt, the kidneys give up on you."

"And I hear that's *terrible* for your skin," I said. The table laughed and I shut my mouth for the majority of the afternoon after that, so I wouldn't spoil my victory.

Instead of running my mouth, upon retiring for the napping hour after lunch, I ran my pen in a friendly letter to Sherlock Holmes. Short and sweet, here it is.

> *Dear Mr. Holmes,*
> *Mr. Watson and I are in your neighborhood, more or less. Should you like to say hello in person, there is a party happening on the 15th at the return address. You may have to put up with a little celebrity admiration, unless you come in a very convincing costume. My cousin is being adopted by a woman who's at least a year younger than her but far more worldly, a way to solidify their 'Boston marriage' as she's referred to it. I spent time in America and yet have never heard the phrase before, have you? Please educate me by letter if you aren't able to do so in person.*
> *Your friend,*
> *Mrs. Watson*

February 14th 1924

Yesterday was a doozy. George and Mellie put us to work. Placing tables, surrounding them with chairs, decorating the tables, counting the silverware. Obviously the bulk of the work was done by hired help, but Watson and I with our soft hands and advanced age were tired by any amount of participation nonetheless. It was good to do the majority of the setup yesterday however, for today we all shared a lovely Valentine's Day dinner, just the four of us, on the eve of all becoming family by law.

As far as my curiosity on the relationship between Mellie and George, I can't really be sure. Because I know that my husband and his roommate-turned-partner were far more than that to one another, I worry that I may be projecting my experience onto my cousin and her friend. Perhaps George aims to be husband material, but that doesn't mean that Mellie has signed on to be a wife in all aspects. Perhaps George is only as she is because, like many women who must run the business affairs of an estate, she has realized that a male name and dress get her taken more seriously; this is no maid in need of a man, but an independent woman, full stop. Or maybe it's everything I suspect, and George and Mellie are fully in love. Perhaps they join one another in bed each night and are far more like a truly wed couple than even Watson and I, who are often mistaken as brother and sister and live very much in that fashion.

Either way, it isn't a question I will ask explicitly, first of all because it doesn't matter to me who Mellie loves so long as she's loved in return, happy, and healthy. Second of all, the secret of my marriage is more Watson's secret than mine, and it's wiser to keep it in-house, though I'd trust Mellie with anything of mine in a heartbeat should it ever become necessary to be radically honest.

I'm tired. Must get to bed early in the hopes that I shall be restored for the festivities tomorrow. Will update with any and all gossip and/or merriment that I experience after the party.

February 15th 1924

Where to begin? I guess I shall break it down by the hour.

6 AM—I was up for breakfast with Mellie, just me and her in the early dawn as Watson slept in later and George was delegating final touches on the party. We ate a spare breakfast of toast and tea knowing there would be plenty of food to indulge in later, and I asked her the most forward question I dared which was, "Once the papers are signed, dear, how will you consider George? Mother or father? Brother, sister, husband, wife?"

Mellie only smiled at me like I was testing her on a secret we swore we'd never speak about again, long ago. Her only answer was to say, "When the guests are gone, we're going to exchange rings. You and Mr. Watson may witness that if it wouldn't offend either of you?" I took her ringless hand and told her firmly, "We'd be honored."

11 AM—After helping as much as I could in checking up on little things (like whether the pen for the guest book had enough ink), I freshened up and changed into my party clothes with Watson. I told him about the private ring ceremony and the thought of it nearly rendered him speechless with emotion. I think we both understand that we're here for something far more special and intimate than a strange adoption and a silly party.

He didn't know that I'd written to Holmes and I wouldn't tell him about it unless and until the man himself actually arrived, which would depend on whether my note reached Holmes in enough time, and if he then felt inclined to travel. I like to see Watson happy but hate to get his hopes up, and I know enough about Holmes not to count on him for social niceties. If there's true danger to combat, Holmes is reliable, but if he's late to tea, don't hold it for him.

1 PM—The party began with assigned seating for lunch, with dancing and mingling to follow after the adoption paperwork was finalized and notarized before a room of witnesses. A photographer was there to capture the moment, and whisked George and Mellie away for a few more pictures in scenic areas outdoors.

This is when coffee and alcohol made the rounds for attendees, and I asked for a good helping of brandy because I'd been at the relatives table, seated beside George's brother-in-law (Willard), and Mellie was right—he was absolutely vile.

"Can you believe this? All to hand the family wealth over to an outsider instead of her own flesh and blood," he griped.

I made sure I was chewing something every time he looked to me for agreement. His wife, George's sister Louisa, sat silent and stoic, as if she had mentally transcended to a peaceful place where her husband's complaints could not be heard any louder than the whine of an insect's wings.

"It just seems insulting, not to me of course," Willard insisted. "Since I can support my own children, naturally, but to snub her only sister's children when Georgina clearly isn't planning on having any of her own, it just seems heartless. And to throw a party about such an aberrant decision, I just wonder about her mental state, I really do."

I bet he does, I bet he would love to put his sister-in-law in an asylum and take over everything she'd built herself.

"George," I told him. "I believe she goes by George in business and in life."

"Who are you again?" he asked me, with acid in his voice.

"A friend of the family," I told him, smiling wide in the hopes that the berry pie I was enjoying at the time made my teeth look bloody.

"Right, well her name is actually Georgina and I don't see any harm in calling her by the name her mother gave her," Willard said, waving a hand dismissively.

"I'm sure you don't," I said, sarcasm oozing like the cherry filling through my teeth.

3 PM—Guess who was fashionably late? Sherlock Holmes arrived just as the first of the invited guests were leaving. He brought the answer to my question about the phrase 'Boston marriage' with a gift for the happy pair—a copy of the Henry James novel *The Bostonians*.

Though Holmes says the book doesn't use the exact phrase itself (much like my husband never wrote the phrase "Elementary, my dear Watson" in his stories, though people frequently quote it to him as if he had), the novel is nevertheless a story about two women who meet over feminist activism and move in together to study, better themselves, and prepare for the fight for equality. Those plans derail when one of the women marries the male cousin of the other, and while Mr. James wasn't exactly endorsing the message of feminism in his portrayal, the story still tells people about an alternative sort of union between independent women, and has helped popularize the name 'Boston marriage' to identify it. To name something gives it power, that is why the contract of adoption signed today is so important: it labels two women as family members who before were just friends, associates, and housemates.

Willard was consumed with jealousy that George and Mellie could draw such a well-renowned guest as Sherlock Holmes.

"It's quite an honor to meet you," Willard said to Holmes, before introducing his wife but not getting out of the way to let her make her hello. "I must say, though..." Willard leaned close to Holmes, and clapped an intrusive hand on his shoulder as if they were old pals. Holmes looked at the hand and then at its owner with mild disgust. "I'm surprised you keep such unusual friends."

"I have had nothing but unusual friends," Holmes told him, before looking toward Watson to find a way out of the crowd, and out from under Willard's heavy hand. "I'm an unusual friend myself."

With that Watson intervened, leading our esteemed detective away to refresh himself after his journey. It was only then that Willard realized that my Watson was *the* Watson, that I was the cousin of Mellie's who married him, and looked at me as if I'd lied to him when I merely let him make his own foolish assumptions.

I didn't like the way he squinted at me, then Mellie, then George. He doesn't seem like a smart man, but I don't doubt he could scheme up something unpleasant for us all.

Holmes and Watson disappeared until dinner. George went off to have cigars with some business associates, and Mellie and I kicked off our shoes in the demolished dining area as the catering staff revolved around the tables like bees among flowers, clearing the dishes.

I asked Mellie if she was happy. She said, "Happy? I'm euphoric."

I teased her by calling her Euphoric until we decided we could both use an afternoon nap.

8 PM—It was only during a late, light dinner (after rings and a sealing kiss were exchanged in hushed, holy silence) that Mellie and George got a full blast of Mr. Sherlock Holmes. We ate some cold sandwiches out of the day's leftovers, and Watson wound up his friend like a clockwork toy and let him regale our hosts with his tricks.

Holmes told George that she went to school in Edinburgh—true! She was inspired by the Edinburgh Seven who in 1869 were the first group of female medical students to matriculate in undergraduate classes at a British university.

Holmes told Mellie that she crocheted but did not knit, another fact that he discerned somehow from the way she held her knife.

He dazzled all of us by saying the dining room we sat in was originally begun as a chapel, but for whatever reason was quickly altered into the august presentation space it was used for today and in all living and historical memory. Something to do with the ceilings, he said; only George was particularly interested in these details, as Watson and I have learned to simply swallow whole what Holmes tells us.

Holmes, though invited at the last minute, sang well for his supper and was prepared a room down the hall from Watson and myself. It was there I went later to collect Watson for our bedtime.

10 PM—After stomping my way down the hall and knocking loud enough to wake the dead, Holmes answered the door and bowed me through. Watson was sitting casually on Holmes's bed, poring over a scattering of newspaper clippings. He seemed to be putting them in chronological order before he saw me and said, "What an incredible woman."

"Thank you?" I asked him. Holmes smirked at us both.

"He is speaking of Nell Pickerell," Holmes told me. "I happened to have collected some amusing stories, sent to me by an associate in the Pacific Northwest region of the United States. I don't know your cousin or her friend well enough to know if they'd enjoy such stories, and so shall give them instead to the Watsons to do with as they see fit."

"More than friend," I said. "George is technically my cousin's mother now, isn't she, which makes her my auntie?" I felt my eyes jitter around in my head for a moment, boggled by the mess of it all, before shrugging the whole matter off my mind. That's all paperwork, really; I will most assuredly never address anyone as Auntie George.

I perused some of the headlines and opening paragraphs in Holmes's news clippings and became quickly fascinated. Here are some of the highlights.

> April 20th 1900—*In Male Attire; "Harry Livingston" Says She Will Wear Them: A Masquerading Girl Gave the Police a Good Run Last Night. May Go to Nome.*

> April 30th 1900—*This Girl Refuses to Wear Skirts; Nellie Pickerell Acts, Talks and Dresses Like a Man, and says She Ought to Have Been One.*

> May 12th 1900—*A Woman By Nature—A Man By Choice: Miss Nellie Pickerell Discards Skirts When a Girl and Adopting a Man's Name, Dresses Like a Man Acts Like a Man and Associates Entirely With Men.*

That last one tells one pretty clearly that headlines are not to be trusted. First of all, if Pickerell went by Harry Livingston, or Livingstone, or as other stories state, Harry Allen, then why was it always "Nellie" who made the paper? More importantly, if Pickerell associated "entirely" with men, then what of this next scandalous batch of news?

December 26th 1901—*Suicide Ends the Love Affair.* Dolly Quappe took a dose of carbolic acid and died from its effects this afternoon. She loved Nell Pickerell, whom she believed to be a boy. The Pickerell girl masquerades in men's clothing and has won the hearts of several susceptible girls. The Quappe girl was a waitress. She came here from Portland, where her mother lives.

November 4th 1903—*Girl Tries To End Her Life; Pearl Waldron Falls in Love With Notorious Nell Pickerell.* The latest victim of a mad infatuation for the Pickerell woman, who goes under the name of Harry Livingstone, is Pearl Waldron, who last night shot herself, inflicting a wound which will probably prove fatal. In March, 1902, Hazel Walters, a young woman of respectable parentage, committed suicide by swallowing carbolic acid. Her discovery that Livingstone was a woman caused her to take her life. It is not known whether such a discovery was responsible for Miss Waldron's attempt to end her life, though it is certain her attachment for the Pickerell woman is what led up to her effort at self-destruction.

July 1st 1915—*Two Girls Died for Love of Man-Woman; She Has Been Cowboy and*

Miner and Can Fight Like a Champion.
Two girls have committed suicide for love
of her. Gertie Samuels shot herself in the
temple when "Harry" failed to show up at
the church. Hazel Walters left a note, "I love
you, 'Harry,' though you are a living lie,"
and hurled herself off a cliff at Madrona
park when she made the discovery that
"Harry" was a woman. When Nell was
arrested this time, the police found her in
a saloon in company with a man and two
girls, drinking. Neither the man nor the
girls suspected that Nell was not a man.

So many women, some dying twice in two different manners for the love of Pickerell, amazing. There was even a mention of one Isabelle Maxwell, a prostitute whom Pickerell called "wife," who was the reason Pickerell was arrested under the Mann Act, the White-Slave Traffic Act, for transporting Maxwell across state lines for immoral purposes.

In addition to reportedly being "a cowboy, a bartender and a miner in her time," Pickerell was also called "a 'pool slicker' of merit," and was often arrested in connection with thefts and brawling.

*February 21st 1906—Police Baffled By
Silence Of A Nervy Young Woman; Female
After Month's Imprisonment Refuses to
Tell What She Knows About Big Robbery.*

*January 21st 1908—Nell Pickerell in a
Tacoma Strongbox; Girl Who Insists
on Wearing Men's Clothes is Believed
to be Member of Dangerous Gang.*

While the papers speculated wildly, there was one thing Pickerell was clear about in every speech or interview.

> November 22ᵈ 1911—*Nell Pickerell Denies Her Sex; Woman Who Dresses in Male Attire Starts Story She is a "Real Man"; Rumor Causes Sensation; Sheriff Stone Brands Statement an Untrue Fabrication Result of Liquor.*

After so much "marrying" women and fighting men and even biting a police officer, after surviving a knife fight with Robert Pickerell, father of Nell, our sensational Pickerell died at roughly forty years old from illness, syphilitic meningitis.

> December 28ᵗʰ 1922—**PICKERELL—** *Funeral services for Nell Pickerell will take place from the Butterworth mortuary, 1921 First Ave., Saturday, Dec. 30, at 4 p.m. All friends invited. Cremation.*

I was stunned, mouth slightly agape, following the timeline beside my dear Watson. When Holmes saw that I had reached the end of the story, he explained.

"You can see why your cousin's ceremony here to George Addington, of all peculiar women, made me think of Nell Pickerell, but not knowing if they'd find this collection an appropriate gift for the occasion, I decided I would introduce these stories to yourself and Watson first."

A wise call if he'd ever made one. After a bit of study ourselves, I will give the pages to Mellie first, and she can be the last one to choose whether they belong to George or not.

February 16th 1924

Not only did George enjoy the wild and unlikely (and clearly only partially true) stories of "Nell" Pickerell, she also regaled Holmes, Watson, and myself with another similar situation.

Apparently George had heard tell of an independent woman named Anne Lister, who often was called 'Gentleman Jack' in the early 1800s, for she dressed more like a man as well, and took her companions exclusively from the fairer sex.

"I have it on good authority that Lister was a prodigious diary keeper," George told us. "She put the good stuff in code, called it writing in 'crypt hand' so that only she could decipher it."

That reminded me of something Oscar Wilde said, and so I repeated it. "I never travel without my diary. One should always have something sensational to read in the train."

Again I got at least a smile (Holmes) if not an outright guffaw (George) from the entire dinner table, and clammed up again to listen, basking in my borrowed comedic success.

"Lister caught a fever from a tick bite and died before age fifty," George continued. "The woman she considered herself married to brought the body back to England for burial. After that woman's death, a distant relative, John Lister, inherited their home, Shibden Hall, and it is his son who has apparently cracked the code. However, in order to avoid attention for his own... let's call it sentiment towards the unfair sex, which is how I refer to men—no offense, gentlemen—Mr. Lister won't let those diaries be known too far or wide any time soon. I have had a preview, though. Here, let's see if Mr. Holmes appreciates this cipher."

George sketched out some code on a napkin, and handed it to Holmes first. As the great Holmes brought the note close to his aging eyes and scrutinized it, George continued.

"Mr. Lister and his friend found the key in a four-letter word, 'hope.' After that, they were able to work out the rest."

Holmes raised his eyebrows, and passed the napkin to Watson next, who shared it with me. At the top, it had the 'hope' key

(Ø5†3=HOPE) and then a string of what looked to me like Greek and mathematical symbols.

Holmes was able to decipher it, and later told Watson, who told me. It said, "I love and only love the fairer sex, and thus beloved by them in turn, my heart revolts from any love but theirs."

An eyebrow-raiser indeed.

February 17th 1924

Holmes left early this morning. I suspect he only stayed the weekend because I've been so preoccupied with my Mellie reunion that he's had Watson to himself. However, he didn't disappear without a few last little treats for us all.

First, there was one more figure of the recent past that he shared with Watson and me as he put on his traveling garb, before heading downstairs to say goodbye to Mellie and George.

"There was a woman born in Ireland who dressed as a boy and stowed away to the United States," Holmes said. "There, as a man named Albert D.J. Cashier, he served in the Civil War in multiple battles. Unwounded and honorably discharged, he lived out his days on a soldier's pension, worked as a handyman and farmhand, and led the parade on Decoration Day each year for memorializing and honoring those soldiers who died in battle. In the end he arrived at the Soldier's and Sailor's old age home, ready to retire in peace."

That sounded like a beautiful ending to an inspiring story, but Watson and I waited. We both knew a Holmes flourish-finish when we heard one, and so knew that this story was not over.

Holmes clasped his bag shut, but did not pick it up. He turned to us to complete his tale.

"While at this home where Cashier should have found an old soldier's final rest, they at long last discovered the girl from Ireland that he once was. On realizing this, they decided Private Cashier had been an insane woman named Jennie Hodgers the whole time, moved him to a mental asylum, and insisted he look the part by wearing dresses and nightgowns. Cashier tripped on the hem of one of these garments, and it was the fall that killed him."

"No," I ejaculated, denying it though I knew it was true. Life was often far more ironic and dramatic than fiction, usually in cruel, petty ways like that.

Watson just shook his head, the same way he did whenever anything went terribly wrong—an election, a storm, a medical diagnosis—that he disagreed with deeply but could do nothing to change.

Holmes smiled at the sad pair he had created. "It is an interesting story, but didn't seem appropriate for your friends on their happy weekend. If it's any consulation, The Grand Army of the Republic, a fraternity of veterans who'd served the Union during the Civil War, made sure that Cashier's burial came with full military honors."

"Fraternity," I repeated, finding it to be the key word that almost unlocked a happy ending. I looked toward Watson to see if he agreed.

"A group for men, brothers," Watson said with a nod.

So despite the tragedy, Cashier's brothers-in-arms didn't forget him. Watson took my hand, and I gave him a smile, and Holmes sighed and said he really had to get back to the very important business of retirement (I'm paraphrasing).

As much as that story wasn't for Mellie and George, Holmes did have a parting tale for them as well, as they all shook hands and told Holmes what an honor it was to meet, and host, and gaze upon the body that held his glorious brain (again, paraphrasing, but not much).

"That brother I met at your party," he said to George.

"Brother-in-law," George said, with a grim nod.

"He'd like to be trouble for you both, and if he ever gets up the courage..."

"Which is no guarantee," George said.

"Right, but if he does, this will disarm him."

Holmes slipped a note from his pocket and handed it to George. He lifted Mellie's hand, tipped his hat to me, and squeezed Watson's shoulder. Then he was out the door and down to the street and on his own way again.

George opened the note, read it, and smirked. "According to Mr. Holmes, Willard has a gambling problem."

"Oh my!" Mellie said with glee, a big smile on her face, the same she had as a kid when it was time for dessert.

Watson and I shared a look with one another, pleased but unsurprised that Holmes would know everything useful under the sun.

"Did he explain his reasoning?" Watson asked, forever noting the Holmesian method of deduction.

George skimmed the page for us. "He says Willard's fretting about money, coupled with the threadbare nature of their finest clothes might lead anyone to suspect financial troubles, but, and I quote, 'the revealing culprit behind their precarious finances was the dusting of card table felt on his suit jacket.' Bravo."

"A little proof of that could get him out of our hair," Mellie said.

George nodded. "I have an investigator I can trust, that will be item one tomorrow morning."

"After we have a great, big goodbye breakfast for our guests?" Mellie asked, reminding George that the Watsons were still loitering in their front hall.

"Of course," George said, her hands opening magnanimously. "We are family, after all."

The Pathétique Symphony

August 22nd 1928

In these wild and roaring '20s, this old gal has spent the better part of a week smashing up chipped plates and cups and other imperfect ceramics with the intention of making a mosaic backsplash just above the fireplace. It may come to naught, it's already become an overwhelming project (first smash, then select the best pieces, then grind down any lethally sharp edges, and then sort by color for future art-making), but in these last dragging days of summer, there's really nothing else to do. The air's too thick to think or read, the day too bright to abide, and so I sit in the shade with a hammer, chisel, and some sandpaper, and make an organized mess.

It's not all drudgery though, Watson has gotten a letter from Holmes (happy husband, happy home), and in it was an invitation to both of us to attend a music performance in London next month. Sounds lovely to me, I'm already imagining September city streets, being bundled up in an orchestra hall, and dining at the Savoy. Did I mention we'd be staying at the Savoy? Holmes's name, when he chooses to drop it, opens a lot of doors, and the Watsons are to be his honored guests.

In this summer funk, I can't think of anything more lovely than sweeping into a high-ceilinged room with autumnal air trailing behind me like a bridal train.

September 16th 1928

Ah, London. Though it stinks as only cities can and I am out of practice at walking as fast as city-dwellers move, it still feels refreshing to get out of the house and have things to do. Music and culture, a reason to get dressed up for dinner, places to be and art to appreciate. Not that I'd want to leave my peaceful little home with Watson altogether, but a change is as good as a rest sometimes, and this brisk trip will make coming home welcoming again, instead of just a matter of course.

The Savoy is a glorious building, already filthy with history at the ripe old age of forty or so. Watson and I had our bags escorted alongside us by a bellhop as we entered. We walked across the mesmerizing checkered floor tiles and past mammoth columns to get to the check-in desk. Watson gave Holmes's name before giving his own, and the man behind the desk didn't flinch, probably trained to show neither disgust nor deep interest towards anyone famous who came to stay. We were taken up to a suite which overlooked the river, and were left alone to ooh and aah and unpack for half an hour before someone rapped smartly at the door.

It was Holmes, of course. I fluffed some pillows while he and Watson hugged hello, and by the time I looked up they were moving as casually around each other as if they'd met for lunch just the day before. Their old habits return so quickly it would be intimidating if I didn't know that my place as Watson's wife was a place Holmes never could or would want to occupy.

The first item of business was getting dressed for dinner.

You can't eat in just any old thing at the Savoy, even on a Sunday night. Watson and I knew we'd need fancy dress for the London Symphony Orchestra performance, and we donned those costumes for dinner in the main dining hall.

Rows of white linen tablecloths, billowing in the breeze of every passerby like the fluttering skirts of dancers. Everyone looked glamorous even if they were not; we were all famous in the golden lights, with crisp waiters waltzing to and fro.

Holmes ordered us all the tasting menu. He told us stories about how the music conductors were in flux these days, how much London wanted to compete with Berlin's symphonies. He also told us we would be hearing Tchaikovsky's Sixth Symphony, also known as his Pathétique Symphony. Apparently since Tchaikovsky's death in 1893 his work has really come back into vogue, enjoying regular performances before the war. In fact, there was once a weekly Tchaikovsky night at the Queen's Hall, where we'll be attending our performance tomorrow. Somehow old Pyotr could still draw the crowds.

I munched away at my food as Holmes spoke and Watson asked questions. I tried to think of a way to get as much of the tasty sauces off my dish and into my mouth without licking the plate outright. I felt as if that sort of behavior would get us looked down upon, just one of those womanly intuitive moments, you know.

It was around then when Watson announced, "Well, this is all so fascinating, I feel as if I could stay up all night hearing about it, but of course that wouldn't be fair to you, dear." That's me, I'm dear.

Holmes suggested, "Well, we could always let Mrs. Watson rest in my room. It's on a higher floor with a more sweeping view, and that way our discussions wouldn't disturb her."

It was all so carefully phrased it was as if they'd planned it before, and maybe they had, or maybe they were just of the same mind, as they often were during their better days. Clearly they both wanted the same thing tonight.

It stung, but I smiled through the wince and said, "What a great idea."

I now record this in what should have been Holmes's room, as Holmes shares my Watson's bed. I'll do my best to dream of the massive breakfast I'll have all to myself in here, instead of whatever is happening between my husband and his old friend in there.

September 17th 1928

I'm enjoying my coffee next to the demolished remains of what used to be an Omelette Arnold Bennett, recently named after the author, whom the bellhop said was a frequent *habitué* here (that's French for he comes around a lot). The omelette had smoked haddock, hard Cheddar cheese, and creamy sauce. It was heavy enough to hold me until dinner, I expect.

The bellhop had expected Sherlock Holmes to be in his own room, and he was suspicious until he heard my name was Mrs. Watson.

"Oh, I see," he said with a nod. "Holmes and Watson must be working a case from the other room, and you're helping to provide cover, is that it?"

"Sounds plausible enough, doesn't it?" I asked. I was happy when this young man left with a tip that would make him think fondly on all of us for the rest of his life. I wonder what stories he'll imagine and tell of the week-long Savoy Scuffle case that never existed.

September 18th 1928

Last night was... remarkable.

Firstly, what I don't know about music can fill all the songbooks in all the world, but I liked it. Tchaikovsky's Sixth Symphony was sweeping and beautiful and certainly long enough to allow me to contemplate its other name, the Pathétique Symphony, and how that is a kind of mistranslation from Tchaikovsky's original Russian. Tchaikovsky called it the Pateticheskaya Symphony, as in 'passionate' or 'emotional,' from which the French took to mean pathétique, as in 'emotive' and in their case, solemn. And here we are at the end of the line, a largely English audience in London, wondering what's so pathetic about such grand music. From Slavic to Romance to Germanic, the words don't communicate perfectly, but the music certainly does.

On our river walk after the performance to cool down, collect our thoughts, and keep the magic of the night going a little longer, I suggested that music could be a universal language.

"Or not universal, but world-wide, universal among humankind on earth," I said, thinking I had saved myself from being corrected by Holmes, but there may never be a day like that for me.

"Music is too culturally linked," Holmes said, and as with every subject, if he wasn't *the* expert, he was certainly more expert than Watson or I in most things, in objective things. I've got the both of them beat on subjective intelligence, but I find that's often true when it comes to the difference between men and women in general.

"You mean to say that to some, drums may be a cheerful sound, and to others it would sound sad?" Watson suggested. "Do drums mean marching and war and funerals, or dancing and the pomp of royalty?"

"Something like that," Holmes said. "If you were to select a mournful piece of music and ask a Japanese or an African man to do the same, you may all three surprise one another."

Fascinating stuff, I'm sure. We strolled by the River Thames in the murky city glow, near air that sounded bigger because it was near water (over which sounds carries so much farther). I wondered if Holmes had ever brought a Japanese and an African man together for an intimate exchange of music, but that is not a question I would ask aloud.

"Is there a universal language?" I asked instead.

"The language of physics is the closest we've come," Holmes said. "Meaning mathematics."

"That's no shock, Sherlock," I blurted before I could help myself, because sometimes his habit of explaining simple things that we mere mortals already know feels insulting. I quickly smiled to try and play it off as fun, good-natured ribbing. Rats scurried in the shadows around us—they were the size of human forearms, I swear.

Holmes didn't reply with anything but a nod. I let him spend the night with my husband, I think the least I can get is some leeway in my tone.

I had another question, the answer to which I suspected I already knew somewhere, intuitively once again.

I squeezed Watson's hand as I said, "Was Tchaikovsky ever married?"

"He was," Holmes said.

"And was it a happy marriage?" I asked.

"It was not," Holmes said.

Which then begged the next question I had. "Was there any particular reason for that?"

Then Watson squeezed my hand back and Holmes sighed. "There was," he said. "If you'd like to hear the details, I suggest we retire somewhere more private for a nightcap."

"Watson?" I asked. As curious as I was, about Tchaikovsky and what his music might mean to Holmes and men like him, I wouldn't insist on being a third wheel on their bicycle built for two if Watson didn't want me there, and so I gave him a chance to say so.

"Sounds good to me," Watson said. "The poor Americans are suffering under prohibition still, we can start by drinking to them."

"Oh, to be sober in America, what a tragedy," Holmes said, and having lived so many of my developmental years doing just that, being sober and studious in the United States, I laughed, because I concurred.

Funnily enough, the bar in the Savoy is called the American Bar, not because it wants to be full of expatriates from across the pond (though it often is), but because when it was first opened in the gay '90s, an American bar was any one serving mixed American-style drinks, i.e. cocktails. In honor of that, I ordered what the bar tender said was the first cocktail ever invented, the Sazerac. Originating from New Orleans, it's a variation of a cognac or whiskey cocktail, so-called because of the Sazerac de Forge et Fils brand of cognac brandy that was its original main ingredient. My drink had rye whiskey, bitters, and sugar in it, as well as absinthe, but not the banned kind apparently, not the kind that gave poets visions. Instead I got the color and flavor of what used to be quite a third-eye-opening experience. Also there was a lemon twist.

The men and I were able to secure a little table to ourselves, and there we could speak freely, so long as we did so quietly, in a huddle over our drinks.

"So, about Tchaikovsky's unhappy marriage," I prompted.

Holmes leaned in over our tiny round table, and started from the beginning.

"Pyotr Tchaikovsky had relationships with men as far back as his student days in St. Petersburg, but being unable to find the full breadth of love with other men, he was never fully satisfied."

I've never been fully satisfied with love either, but I sipped my drink and let the men carry the conversation.

Watson said, "Did he marry for want of love then?"

"Oh, no," Holmes said, shaking his head. "In fact, he told his younger brother Modest, who also had these same inclinations towards his own kind, quite explicitly, 'I seek marriage or some sort of public involvement with a woman so as to shut the mouths of assorted contemptible creatures.'"

"An arranged marriage," I said. "Arranged by rumors and paranoia."

"More or less," Holmes said, sipping his own whiskey and soda. "His first attempt at matrimony was with Belgian soprano Désirée Artôt, whom he met in 1868. They became rather infatuated with one another, were engaged to be married, but as her mother vehemently opposed Artôt marrying someone seven years her junior, and because Artôt refused to give up stage performing and move to settle in Russia with Tchaikovsky, the marriage never came to be. Tchaikovsky considered her to be the only woman he ever loved, the only woman he actually wanted to marry."

"And then he married someone else?" Watson asked.

"He did," Holmes said.

"Lucky girl," I said, trying not to sound too bitter. I myself am a second wife, and if Watson was truly in love with anyone at this table only to be thwarted by circumstances outside his control, it wasn't me.

After a beat, Holmes continued. "Her name was Antonina Miliukova, a former student that he married in July of 1877, and never saw again after September of 1877."

I laughed aloud, somehow I couldn't help it. An absolute ass's bray, other tables looked around and judged me uncouth before shaking their heads and returning to their own conversations.

"Three months?" I asked. "They only made it three months?"

"Two and a half," corrected Holmes, amused at my reaction. The alcohol must have gone straight to my head.

"Did she leave him?" Watson asked.

"He left her," Holmes said. "Tchaikovsky told his new bride that someone was waiting for him in St. Petersburg, he left on the 24th of September, and never saw her again."

"Probably for the best," I said. "I doubt he was very good company at home."

"Tchaikovsky came to the same conclusion," Holmes said. "He wrote to his patron, a woman named Madame Nadezhda Von Meck whom he never met in person but corresponded with voluminously throughout the years, that he was by nature a savage, and at his best when he was alone."

"It's rather sad to be alone though," Watson said. There was a reason he married me and I married him: neither of us wants to be alone, and together we make for fine companions and agreeable housemates. We know exactly how the other takes their tea, what size we each wear, how best to wake one another each morning. Little familiarities like that really do make a life together, and if they don't quite reach the level of a passionate symphony, they are still a form of love.

"Oh, he wasn't exactly alone, he was only done seeking the company of women," Holmes said, before finishing his drink, checking his watch, and moving as if to stand. "I shall tell the rest of what I know tomorrow perhaps?"

"What is tomorrow, what shall we do?" I asked. "When will you gentleman come fetch me from my tower?"

I knew they'd want to spend all our nights in London together, and figured I might as well let them know I'd allow it. I think of it not as their time together, but as my time to myself to sleep sprawled with abandon in bed and to reach my own ends, to put it delicately—to really luxuriate in my own fantasies and passions, if you know what I mean.

That is what's on my menu tonight, and tomorrow we'll spend the afternoon at the British Museum.

September 19th 1928

Today was sunny, dry, and cool, the last bit of temperate weather before winter is truly upon us. At approximately 10 o'clock in the morning, after breakfast and plenty of time to put some interesting twists in my hair, I was summoned by bellhop to the lobby where my escorts awaited me.

"Lovely, darling," Watson said as I took his arm, and he noticed my effort with curls and pins.

There's a very fine chance that Holmes only noticed my hair enough to register that there was a bejeweled comb stuck in the thick of it, in case it was stolen, or I was stolen and its description would help aid in solving the case. It has small pearls affixed to gold leaves like berries, and at the center a cameo of a hummingbird. It used to be my mother's, and though she died when I was quite young I remember seeing it in her hair, and that either the hummingbird was her favorite type of bird, or the angel's trumpet flowers it suckled from were her favorite type of flower. Or both could be true, I never had the chance to ask her.

The British Museum was hardly a ten-minute walk past churches and gardens, theaters and clubs. Soon we were in the shadow of its Greek Revival façade and towering Ionic columns, ready to see what the empire had dragged back from the world for us to admire.

First up: two gold medallions of Constantius Chlorus found recently in a brickfield where they'd been buried some time in the fourth century. Next: a marble relief of Aeneas at the site of Rome. Following that: the hall collection which was comprised of eighty-six items of Greek antiquity, bequeathed after the death of a private collector's widow. The crowning items there were a few pre-Etruscan bronze urns in excellent condition.

Then it was on to an Egyptian sphinx dedicated by King Amenemhet IV, the last king of the Twelfth Dynasty. After that, Egyptian cuneiform tablets, then other assorted treasures of Rome, a smattering of early English and Anglo-Saxon antiquities, and a Persian pottery bowl. Holmes, Watson, and I moved quietly and somberly through each of these exhibits, until we found ourselves in front of a selection of Greek coins, and somehow that inevitably led to murmurs of Lord Byron, who died for Greece's war of independence in Missolonghi on April 19, 1824 at the age of thirty-six, after living for little more than pleasure, poetry, and scandal. He fell in love with women, sired daughters, but in the end died in the arms of his fourteen-year-old Greek lover Nicolo Giraud. At least he fit a lot of life into his short years on this earth, a lot of passion.

By the time we reached showings of diplomatic papers, a letter from Charles Dickens to 'George Eliot,' and a particularly grand copy of *Don Quixote* from the Ashendene Press in Chelsea printed on vellum, we were ready for lunch.

We ended up at one of London's oldest (if not *the* oldest, full stop) restaurant, Rules. Opened near Covent Gardens on church grounds by Thomas Rule in 1798, it began as primarily an oyster bar, but has a full spread of traditional British cuisine. It has a disarmingly country feel for a city establishment.

Watson ordered a helping of shepherd's pie, Holmes a bowl of rabbit stew, and I myself selected a Dorset crab salad. We were largely silent as we ate, which is how you know the food was good, and all three of us agreed to retire to the upstairs bar afterwards for desserts, drinks, and coffee. In the end, we each had a bit of all of the above, for we sat there hours.

After ordering our post-meal snacks (sticky toffee pudding for Watson, an Arctic ice cream roll for me, and a scotch quail's egg for Holmes) and finishing a pot of coffee, it was nearing the evening hour and an appropriate time for drinks once again.

Holmes chose a bottle of port wine for the table, but after a quick taste out of Watson's glass, I found the lure of well-mixed cocktails irresistible. I ended up with what the bartender said was The Monkey Gland, named rather rudely after the pseudo-scientific idea that grafting tissue from monkey testicle into humans would increase our longevity. The drink originated from another American bar, the New York Bar in Paris, and it too had absinthe in it, along with gin, orange juice, and grenadine, giving it the appearance of a smoldering sunset.

That got me thinking, as I often do, of something Oscar Wilde said. I liked his plays and witticisms immensely before I ever really spared a thought about his personal life, but considering my personal life and the kind of man I married, I think even more often of him now, nearly thirty years after his death. Though my sympathies will always lie far more heavily with his wife, Wilde did love his children (not all men do) and actually enjoyed the company of strong-willed women, especially actresses (even fewer men can tolerate that). Wilde also appreciated absinthe, or as it was known to him, the Green Fairy.

"Oscar Wilde said the reason that absinthe would drive men mad is because it made them see the world as it really is," I said. "Items taken completely out of context, for example a top hat: men would see such a thing as if for the first time, as if they'd never even heard of the concept of hats before, and that would be maddening."

I was working from a remembered quote, one of Wilde's epigrams. I'll include the original quote below once I get back to my own library:

After the first glass of absinthe you see things as you wish they were. After the second you see them as they are not. Finally you see things as they really are, and that is the most horrible thing in the world. I mean disassociated. Take a top hat. You think you see it as it really is. But you don't because you associate it with other things and ideas. If you had never heard of one before, and suddenly saw it alone, you'd be frightened, or you'd laugh. That is the effect absinthe has, and that is why it drives men mad. Three nights I sat up all night drinking absinthe, and thinking that I was singularly clearheaded and sane. The waiter came in and began watering the sawdust. The most wonderful flowers, tulips, lilies and roses, sprang up, and made a garden in the cafe. "Don't you see them?" I said to him. "Mais non, monsieur, il n'y a rien." [But no, sir, there is nothing.]

Holmes, himself a man who has known substances and the madness they can bring, tipped his head, remembering something. It was like watching him tilt the pool table of his mind, letting the ball of a thought roll into the right pocket.

"He was not the only artist of his time who gained visions from absinthe. You have heard of the poet Paul Verlaine?" Holmes asked.

"I have, I think," I said.

"He lauded absinthe in his youth and condemned it bitterly on his deathbed," Holmes said.

"Wilde became a Catholic on his deathbed," I said. "It seems people feel the need to give up their bad habits before they give up the ghost."

Watson hummed, meaning he found that connection to have some profundity. "Didn't Verlaine's fellow poet and... friend... Arthur Rimbaud find absinthe compelling too?"

Holmes cut his gaze towards me, put one of his long-fingered hands between his face and the rest of the bar, and mouthed the word 'lover' to me.

I nearly snorted my own absinthe drink through my nose.

"He did, as did Byron, Baudelaire, Proust, Poe, and van Gogh," Holmes listed.

"Those wastrels," I said. The liquor had gone to my head and I was having fun, with Holmes of all people.

"Precisely," Holmes said. "Maybe they were right to derange their senses, if it helped fuel and feed their work. Rimbaud called absinthe the 'sagebrush of the glaciers' for its bitter taste, but he gave up both it and poetry at about the same time, for essentially the same reasons."

"He put away childish things," Watson said, nodding along with his educated guess.

Holmes confirmed. "That is how he saw them. He went on to be a pioneer of sorts in Africa, walking places white men had never gone before, making himself a small fortune he was never able to retire on, as he died of bone cancer at age thirty-seven."

"Baby," I said. Everything before forty seems incredibly young to me now.

"Forever the *enfant terrible*, an unruly child of one sort or another to the end," Holmes said. "Verlaine later disavowed absinthe as well, but it took him longer to do so, long enough to contribute to an early death at age fifty-one."

"I guess they earned the name Decadents then," I said. "Did they leave off from each other well?"

"Not at all," Holmes said, signaling for attention from the waiter. "They had such a fight in Brussels that Verlaine put a bullet in Rimbaud's hand and spent some time in jail for it."

"Goodness," Watson said.

"Impressive," I seconded.

"Indeed, they should put up a plaque at that hotel someday marking the occasion," Holmes said as the waiter arrived and he ordered his next drink, this one made of stronger stuff, a Scotch single malt whiskey-based cocktail. I nodded for another Monkey Gland, and Watson waved his hand over his glass to decline, being the most responsible among us today (and most days).

"What would they carve on that plaque?" Watson asked.

"A Season in Hell?" I suggested, knowing the title of Rimbaud's most famous poem.

"Perhaps a more back-handed quote from it," Holmes said. *"Il faut être absolument moderne."*

Translation: *One must be absolutely modern.*

"Was that their last meeting?" I asked.

"They met once more for a final fight after Verlaine got out of prison, they did not mix well," Holmes said, as our drinks were set before us and Watson's water glass refilled.

"They were no cocktail you mean?" I asked.

"Nothing I'd drink," Holmes said.

He took a sip of his new glass and nodded his approval of it. I switched my stirrer from one glass to another and handed the spent cup back to the waiter. After the silence of these transactions passed, it was time for a new topic.

"So about Tchaikovsky's Sixth," I said.

"Right, about that," Holmes said. "It was dedicated to his nephew, the eldest son of his sister Aleksandr and her husband Lev Davidov, a boy who was at least thirty years younger than Pyotr Tchaikovsky. Vladimir Davidov, who went by Bob, was encouraged by his uncle to pursue art and music."

"How did they get 'Bob' out of Vladimir?" I asked.

"When Vladimir was the baby, they called him Baby in English," Holmes said. "But when the baby was unable to pronounce the name correctly himself, he became 'Bob' to all."

"How sweet," Watson said. With his checkered life, Watson never had children, and together he and I haven't managed to acquire any nieces or nephews either. He has quite an avuncular bedside manner with children as a doctor, however; maybe in another life he'd have been a proud papa, but not this one.

"According to Modest Tchaikovsky, brother to Pyotr and Aleksandr, and twin to yet another sibling, Anatoly, Pyotr went from doting uncle to fatherly affection and ultimately to an overwhelming fixation.

He dedicated his Children's Album of piano pieces to Bob in 1878, and his Passionate Symphony to him in 1893."

"So there's the progression of affection," Watson noted. "Fifteen years to go from boy to man."

"Exactly," Holmes said. "Uncle Modest knew of which he spoke. After graduating with a law degree from the Imperial School of Jurisprudence, in 1876 Modest began tutoring a deaf-mute boy named Nikolai, employing a special teaching method that helped him to read, talk, and write. That boy became his longtime companion, and Modest addressed both his and his brother's affections in his still largely unpublished autobiography. As Pyotr's chronicler—"

"His Watson," I said, before piping back down.

"—Modest wrote that, despite the difference in their ages, Pyotr always enjoyed the company of his favorite nephew, but he harangued him in letters while Bob was at school. Overbearing salutations like, *If you do not want to write, at least spit on a piece of paper, put it in an envelope, and send it to me. You are not taking any notice of me at all. God forgive you—all I wanted was a few words from you.*"

Holmes took another sip from his glass, and gazed into its bottom with that signature broodiness he has. I was sympathetic to this mood, however, as what he spoke of didn't seem like a perfectly equal affection between man and boy, did it? Was it ever not dangerously weighted toward one side over the other? Probably not, but especially when it involved family members, which could only make it more fraught.

Holmes continued. "Bob decided on a military career instead of one in the arts, for a time, until he resigned his commission as a lieutenant in 1897, five years after Uncle Pyotr's death. Pyotr was anguished when they were separated, and would confide his most intimate thoughts to Bob in letters, ending each one in increasingly desperate valedictions: *I embrace you, my idol*, exclamation point; *I embrace you with mad tenderness*, full stop; *I embrace you to suffocation*, three exclamation points. He made Bob his principal heir, having no children of his own, and had plans to live with him that never fully came to pass before he died."

"What killed Pyotr?" I asked, suddenly on Christian-name terms with a man I'd never met and, before this trip, had hardly ever thought about. I'm not what you'd call an aficionado of music I can't dance to.

"That depends on who you ask," Holmes said. "It was either a cholera infection from contaminated water, or he poisoned himself to avoid a scandal of the heart involving himself and someone else's nephew. Perhaps cholera was an easier story for everyone to swallow, so to speak."

"Ugh," Watson said, to which I touched his hand in agreement.

"And is Bob still alive?" I asked next.

"He is not," Holmes said. "He shot himself in 1906. He was thirty-five."

Silence at the table, until I said to Holmes, "You're a terrible date."

Watson squeezed my hand (wouldn't he know all about it), and Holmes nodded at me as if acknowledging some grudging compliment.

All that talk of endings, journeys ended in lovers rending, put a wet blanket over our crackling conversation. We finished our drinks, paid our bill, and retired for our final night in London.

September 20th 1928

Here I am, home again. In a lot of ways short trips are perfect: there's hardly time for the dust to settle over the house, there's no need to pause and then unpause the newspaper or the milk deliveries, and we can get back into our normal ruts within hours of return. But that is also the disappointing part of a short trip: as soon as the bags are unpacked it's like we never left at all, as if those visions of London were nothing but a dream, and the memories of our evenings no more than the faintly bitter aftertaste of absinthe on our lips.

Holmes traveled with us upon departure and continued on to his seaside lodgings after Watson and I split off in Crawley. He had some last tidbits of information to distract us from the bumps in the road at least, information about the composition of the Pathétique Symphony and what it has come to mean for so many.

Despite the desperation in Pyotr's letters to his nephew, he tempered his tone when talking about his work, for which he held far more surety and enthusiasm. You can see the change in this excerpt from a letter that Holmes carried a smuggled copy of, dated February 11th 1893.

> *I want to tell you about the excellent state of mind I'm in so far as my works are concerned. You know that I destroyed the symphony I had composed and partly orchestrated in the autumn. And a good thing too! There was nothing of interest in it—an empty play of sounds, without inspiration. Now, on my journey, the idea of a new symphony came to me, this time one with a programme, but a programme that will be a riddle for everyone. Let them try and solve it. The work will be entitled A Programme Symphony (No. 6) Symphonie à Programme (No. 6), Eine Programmsinfonie (Nr. 6).*

It was Modest who suggested the title that was ultimately chosen, *Symphonie Pathétique.*

> *The programme of this symphony is completely saturated with myself and quite often during my journey I cried profusely. Having returned I have settled down to write the sketches and the work is going so intensely, so fast, that the first movement was ready in less than four days, and the others have taken shape in my head. Half of the third movement is also done. There will still be much that is new in the form of this work and the finale is not to be a loud allegro, but the slowest adagio. You cannot imagine my feelings of bliss now that I am convinced that the time has not gone forever, and that I can still work.*

Holmes handed us a few more sheets of paper, copies of intimate correspondence made by whoever sent him this information in the first place, information that presumably prompted him to travel to the nearest performance of this musical composition, and invite the Watsons along with him. There were two other letters behind the February one that also mentioned the Sixth Symphony and featured Pyotr's deep emotional fixation on young Bob.

> *London*
>
> *17-29 May 1893*
>
> *I am writing to you with a voluptuous pleasure. The thought that this paper is going to be in your hands fills me with joy and brings tears to my eyes. Is it not curious that I voluntarily inflict upon myself all these tortures? What the devil do I want it all for? Several times yesterday, on my way, I wanted to run away; but somehow I felt ashamed to return empty-handed. Yesterday my tortures reached such a pitch that I lost both appetite and sleep and this happens very rarely. I am suffering not only from anguish and distress which cannot be expressed in words (in my new symphony there is a place which I think expresses it very well) but also from a vague feeling of fear and the devil only knows what else. The physical symptoms are pains at the bottom of my bowels, and aching and weakness in the legs. So, definitely, this is the last time I am going through all this. From now on I shall agree to go anywhere only for a very large sum of money and not for more than three days...*

> *Klin*
>
> *3 [or 2] August 1893*
>
> *In my last letter to Modest I complain that you don't want to know me, and now he is silent too, and all links with your crowd are completely broken....*

What makes me sad is that you take so little interest in me. Could it be that you are positively a hard egotist? However, forgive me, I won't pester you again. The symphony which I was going to dedicate to you (not so sure that I shall now) is getting on. I am very pleased with the music but not entirely satisfied with the instrumentation. It does not come out as I hoped it would. It will be quite conventional and no surprise if this symphony is abused and unappreciated—that has happened before. But I definitely find it my very best, and in particular the most sincere of all my compositions. I love it as I have never loved any of my musical children.

...At the end of August I shall have to go abroad for a week. If I were sure that you would still be in Verbovka in September I would love to come at the beginning of the month. But I know nothing about you.

I embrace you with all my love.

P. Tchaikovsky

I read them as the wheels rolled beneath us and wondered if Tchaikovsky's Sixth, by whatever name one called it, meant something especially significant for men like Holmes, and in certain lights under certain moons, my dear Watson. Holmes answered the question without my having to ask it, either because he could read my face as easily as he could Watson's, or because it was the only logical question to arrive at with all this information in hand.

"You know of E.M. Forster," Holmes said, more a statement of fact than a question, but he waited for me to respond.

"Of course, *Howard's End,*" I said. "I loved that book, never cried so much over a house."

"He's written another book that won't see the light of day until after he dies, about a man named Maurice who falls in love with another man," Holmes said. "In it, the Pathetic Symphony, as the characters call it, functions as a sort of flirtation between men. The right Wilde phrase or Whitman poem can do the same, but that's neither here nor there, because music is far too easy to misunderstand, especially by those who are uneducated in the nuances."

I held up my hand—I know who I am and I'm comfortable with myself. Holmes nodded, duly noted.

"The flirtation goes right over Maurice's head until someone more in the know clues him in explicitly. After going to a concert of the *Symphonie Pathique*, Maurice insists it's Symphony Pathetic, Philistine that he is, and the other man sets him straight by telling him it's *Symphonie Incestueuse et Pathique* actually, and reveals that Tchaikovsky had fallen in love with his own nephew, and dedicated his masterpiece to the boy."

"It's funny how many people come to hear, never knowing what they've listened to," Watson said.

"It's the queer things we've learned that allow us to know the truth," Holmes said with a shrug.

"I wonder if I'll live to see this book on my library shelf someday," I said. Though I'm younger than Holmes and Watson, we're all far older than we'd prefer.

"Forster wrote the book before the war, between 1913 and 1914," Holmes said, "and that is part of the delay in publication, because he insists that a happy ending for the story is imperative, but the war has left no man perfectly happy."

I nodded, thinking of all my fallen brothers. Watson closed his eyes and crossed himself, as if sending out a silent prayer. Holmes went on.

"Yet another way the happiness of the story is a hindrance to publication is because, while there is no seduction of minors or pornography in its pages, an ending where two men fall in love and remain in it for the 'happily ever after' that only fiction allows… well, that is not allowed, not yet. Forster thinks that if it ended unhappily, with a lad dangling from a noose or with a suicide pact, all would be well, but the lovers get away unpunished and consequently appear to recommend the crime of embracing what they are."

"And embracing one another, I assume," I said.

Holmes nodded. "Forster has decided to dedicate the book to 'a happier year.' If you want to know when it will be published, ask yourself when do you think that happy year will come about?"

"Hopefully this century," Watson said.

"Yes, hopefully," I agreed.

After that, it was nothing more than idle, logistical chatter on our way home, and now Watson and I are thinking our own thoughts in different parts of the house, my part being beside the fireplace, looking upon the shards of that mosaic I still mean to create. The shards are in the same mess they were when I left them, but if what I've learned on this trip has taught me anything, it's that I'll find my inspiration for art whenever I'm consumed by some passionate symphony of emotion that can be expressed in no other acceptable way.

Stalemates

June 25th 1931

Sherlock Holmes doesn't visit often, but when he does, he's usually up for a chess game.

My father taught all of his children to play, including me, "the daughter" as I was often affectionately called. A military man from head to toe, the strategizing in chess fell comfortably under the head game of waging and winning battles for old dad. He never let his children win, which means none of us were able to beat him until we were adults and his mind was fading. I never had the honor myself, though two of my brothers finally got him, and Father and I were in the midst of a long-distance game when he died. I left the game where it was for more than a year after he passed. I often reassemble it when I want to calm my mind; I find doing so soothing, just as my friends find the same peace in putting together a jigsaw puzzle.

It is my dearest wish to someday trounce Holmes at chess. It would make my father grin in his grave. So far, however, that has not been the case. I am long out of practice, and Holmes is Holmes.

Still, when Holmes was on his way back from Cambridge after a consultation of some sort (either *for* him or *from* him—no one tells me the full details) and stopped by to say hello to my Watson, he wondered if we still had a guest room where he was welcome. Where would it have gone, the guest room? It's not as if tornadoes come ripping through West Sussex, snatching rooms from people's houses. It's also not as if Watson and I don't already have more rooms than the two of us can use each day. So yes, Holmes has been allowed to stay, and he may do so for as long as we all can stand it. He's made it for two days and nights so far.

It is in the evenings, after we've all found our own ways to dinner, that the three of us are able to comfortably linger together, waiting until the last light of the day before bed, reading and listening to radio programs and playing our little games. On the first night we all played whist, on the second night I watched Holmes and Watson play chess, whispering hints and suggestions to Watson from behind my book, disrupting Holmes's strategy, though he still won. Tonight he asked to cut out the middle man and play against me and me alone. I didn't want to give him the satisfaction of beating me again—we had many games aboard the ship to and from Australia, all of which I lost, and only a portion of which I lost respectably—but Holmes made me an offer that I found enticing.

"How about for every piece I win, I'll tell you something about a king you've never heard before," Holmes said.

I do love learning, but I also wanted to negotiate harder terms. "What about queens?"

"For the pieces you win from me," Holmes agreed with a nod, his crafty eyes never leaving mine as he tilted his head down.

"Deal," I told him, and so we played.

Now the chess set we have out at arm's length for guests is not my father's set, I keep that far closer to me. The old captain carved the names of each of his children on the underside of the pieces, as well as other names that mattered to him, not all of whom I knew about.

He maxed out on naming the royalty, but not the pawns, a sign of respect I'm sure. My mother was my father's first queen and I was the other, and the rest of the names on the board are sons and men.

The guest set was Watson's old set, possibly one that would have lodged at Baker Street with both of them during their years together. Speaking of Baker Street, I forgot to mention: Arnold Bennett, he of Savoy Grill omelette fame and the novel *A Man from the North*, died there earlier this very spring of typhoid, after drinking some bad tap water in France. H.G. Wells lives at that location now, if you can believe it. I've made the Omelette Arnold Bennett a few times since trying it at the Savoy, and some variations of it with different fish besides smoked haddock. The cream and cheddar are always there though, and of course now an added sense of morbidity.

Anyway, about that chess match: Holmes scored the first casualty, a pawn, and told me something I never knew about King James VI and I (of the Bible translation), and the man he called "wife."

"Wife?" I said, startled and wondering if this devil's bargain I'd made with Holmes wasn't just a tactic to thoroughly distract me and throw me off my chess game.

"Though he was married with children to Anne of Denmark, King James had a number of male favorites, from the age of thirteen when he met Esmé Stewart, his first cousin once removed who was then thirty-seven, and became so infatuated that royal informants reported on the relationship with great concern. 'The King altogether is persuaded and led by him,' they said, 'and is in such love with him as in the open sight of the people often he will clasp him about the neck with his arms and kiss him.' James regularly promoted Stewart until he reached the ultimate rank of Duke of Lennox. The feeling was mutual, as when James eventually was forced to cut ties with Stewart and banish him, Stewart was distressed, writing to James, 'I desire to die rather than to live, fearing that that has been the occasion of your no longer loving me.'"

I took in that information and then tried to compartmentalize it, so I could figure out my next move on the board. Watson, however, had further questions.

"And there were other men he felt that passionately about?"

"Yes, indeed," Holmes said, following my hands with his gaze but speaking freely to Watson. "There was his most beloved, George Villiers, Duke of Buckingham."

He stopped talking as we filled the board back and forth, until he made an extremely inconvenient move for me, threatening one of my bishops. The sneaky man; with such interesting stories, I was almost tempted to sacrifice pieces to get the rest of the information he had.

Holmes continued. "George Villiers was the one he called wife, specifically beginning a letter from 1623 with, 'God bless you, my sweet child and wife, and grant that ye may ever be a comfort to your dear father and husband.'"

"Healthy," I said. I personally like my husband and my father to be completely different people, but maybe I'm too modern.

"He also called him Steenie, for St. Stephen who was said to have an angel's face," Holmes went on. "He also said publicly, to the Privy Council in 1617, 'You may be sure that I love the Earl of Buckingham more than anyone else, and more than you who are here assembled. I wish to speak in my own behalf and not to have it thought to be a defect, for Jesus Christ did the same, and therefore I cannot be blamed. Christ had John, and I have George.' There were rumors, you see, he wanted to get ahead of them."

"By telling everyone else they were nothing to him compared to George, I'm sure that helped appease the public," I said, with a move that won myself a rook. I smiled, for the stories would go on, but this time on my terms.

"It is interesting that he cited the love of Christ to justify his own," Watson said.

"Perhaps that is even why he so desired a new translation of the Bible," I suggested. "He was preparing a defense."

"Well, he had some complaints with the widely-used Geneva translation," Holmes said. "It was too Puritan for him, and had a few marginal notes he disagreed with, particularly one about not executing an idolatrous mother that he felt were targeted at his own mother, Mary, Queen of Scotts."

"So he ordered a whole new kind of Bible," Watson said.

"Such is the privilege of a king," I said. "I like this man, I make him a Duke or an Earl; I don't like this Bible, I say write me another."

"It may not be worth the hanging sword of Damocles," Holmes said, "but being king does have some benefits."

"But tell me about queens," I said, waving my conquered rook. "What were queens able to do?"

"The great-granddaughter of King James, Queen Anne, also had favorites," Holmes said.

"Oh, and numerous unfortunate pregnancies, right?" I asked.

"Yes," Holmes said. "She'd been pregnant at least eighteen times throughout her life, the majority of which resulted in miscarriages or stillborn children. Of the five living children she had, four of them died before they reached the age of two years old, and the remaining son, Prince William, Duke of Gloucester, died at the age of eleven. In a rather nasty irony, she was rendered speechless by a stroke on the exact anniversary of the boy's death fourteen years later, and died the morning after."

"The last of the Stuart monarchs," Watson said. He is also a wealth of information, my Watson, but none of it as secretive and scandalous as what Holmes knows.

Holmes nodded, correct fact acknowledged. "Anne's earliest dalliance with a woman was Mary Cornwallis, about whom Anne's uncle opined that 'no man ever loved his Mistress as Anne did Mrs. Cornwallis.' But it was with Sarah Jennings Churchill, Duchess of Marlborough, that helped change history."

"Because they were in love?" I asked, skeptical because I've learned too much of history to be that optimistic.

"There was certainly deep affection afoot on Anne's part," Holmes said. "She wrote to Sarah with such sentiment as, 'I hope I shall get a moment or two to be with my dear [...] that I may have one dear embrace, which I long for more than I can express.' The queen was always lonely without this particular mistress of the robes and keeper of the privy purse, writing intimacies like, 'I must tell you I am not as you left me... I long to be with you again and tis impossible for you ever to believe how much I love you except you saw my heart.' While she was in the sun, Sarah held great influence over the queen, and even convinced Anne to side with William of Orange in his 1688 Glorious Revolution."

"Didn't that action depose Anne's own father?" Watson asked.

"Ultimately, yes," Holmes said.

Then silence as Holmes held up a hand, squinted at the chess board, and subsequently gathered my threatened bishop. He had to sacrifice his queen to do it, which was the next piece I won, but he was clearly satisfied with the exchange. I wondered what he saw that I didn't, but I often feel that way around Sherlock Holmes.

After this brief conquest, Holmes went on. "William of Orange, married of course to Anne's sister Mary, assumed the throne in 1689. Anne was named as their successor, and she assumed the throne in 1702. She held it until her death, but with no living heir, the seat of power passed over to the Hanoverian descendants of King James I."

"But what about Anne and Sarah?" I asked. If I wanted to learn about the succession of monarchs, I know plenty of former and current teachers I could write to—Holmes owed me the secret history.

"Oh, their relationship cooled after a time, when Anne became more infatuated with Sarah's cousin, Abigail Masham." Holmes sat back and observed our game from a distance while he sipped his tea. "This outraged Sarah, who began spreading rumors about the two, but in the end, her majesty got what she demanded, if not ever exactly what she wanted."

"Just like a king," I said, before realizing I was leaning dramatically forward, rapt with attention to the story and not necessarily the game. Watson was in the same position, but the spell broke for both of us when Holmes agreed with me.

"In some ways, exactly like a king," he said.

Watson popped up from his seat about then to pass around the biscuit tin, full of malted milk, custard cream, and chocolate Bourbon biscuits.

"This," Holmes said as he selected the cream-filled Bourbon cookie (as my American friends would call it) and dunked it in the fresh hot tea Watson poured for us. "This biscuit was rebranded from its original name, Creola. The Garibaldi biscuit people decided that naming it after the French royal House of Bourbon would sell better, and they were right."

"Everyone likes the idea of being royal," Watson said, before putting a Nice biscuit between his teeth and returning to his seat with tea cup in hand. "I don't know that the reality of it would be very satisfying though. They may have more power than us, but we are more free."

"Their days are not their own," Holmes said with a nod.

I crammed a classic digestive in my mouth and washed it down as quickly as possible before getting us back to the topic.

"Speaking of royalty, I believe I'm owed another king?" I asked.

"Edward II," Holmes said. He was eating his biscuit slowly, bite by bite like a gentleman, and I cast my eye over the chessboard at rest as he spoke. "One of our more unsuccessful monarchs, what with the famine he reigned over and the failed invasion of Scotland he drove in 1314, but his ultimate undoing was brought about by squabbling with his barons, a situation that was only inflamed by his relationship with two men: Piers Gaveston and Hugh le Despenser."

"Isn't this…" Watson began. "Didn't Christopher Marlowe write…"

"Oh yes," I remembered. "In the play Edward is killed by some Lucifer-type stand-in, uh, Lightborne?"

"Correct," said Holmes. "The play conflated together a lot of different events, but boldly made the relationship between Edward and Gaveston the central love affair, with Queen Isabella off to the side scheming."

Watson then quoted, "The mightiest kings have had their minions;/ Great Alexander loved Hephaestion,/ The conquering Hercules for Hylas wept;/ And for Patroclus, stern Achilles drooped."

"Goodness," I said. "Wasn't Marlowe killed in a bar brawl?"

"He certainly got a knife in his eye in a bar," Holmes said. "Whether that was a common place dispute over drinks or an assassination ordered by Queen Elizabeth I is still disputed. Even further afield is the idea that Marlowe's death was faked and he secretly wrote a great majority of Shakespeare's output." Holmes shrugged.

"I can believe anything provided it is incredible," I said.

"Oscar Wilde," Watson explained to Holmes. "She's quoting Oscar Wilde again."

"She does do that quite often, yes," Holmes said, before both of them smiled at me like I was their adopted daughter or something.

Holmes brushed his fingers together to get the biscuit crumbs off and leaned forward again over our chess game to examine the state of play, but he kept talking out of one side of his brain even as he plotted my conquer with the other.

"Edward II first met Piers Gaveston as a teenager. His father Edward I banished Gaveston because he didn't like the man's influence on his son. When Edward II took the throne, he brought Gaveston back and made him Earl of Cornwall, which infuriated the noble class because they thought such a title should only be given to royalty, as tradition dictated, but Edward would not be swayed. The revolt of the barons was so dangerous that Gaveston was forced into exile twice, returning each time, until he was captured by the barons and executed in 1312."

"See, it is *not* good to be king," Watson said. I certainly wouldn't take the job.

"It was a few years after this when Edward lost control of Scotland, and his cousin Thomas of Lancaster started leading the opposition against Edward. By that time Edward was also enraptured with and handing out landed positions to Hugh le Despenser and his son, a devotion so clear that the annalist of Newenham Abbey in Devon ultimately referred to them as 'the king and his husband' while others claimed that Despenser had 'bewitched Edward's heart.' The action got quite messy at that point: the Despensers were also banished by the barons, in response to which Edward captured and executed his cousin Thomas in 1322, after which his devotion to the Despensers drove his queen into the arms of an exiled baron by 1325, which then led to the Despensers also being killed and Edward being dethroned. Within a year after that, Edward II died in prison at the age of forty-three, probably not due to natural causes, all things considered."

Watson sighed. Holmes took one of my knights, and I had to move to block his access to my king, which only set me up to lose two more pieces, a pawn and my other bishop. Suddenly my kingdom was eroding and I didn't like it one bit. I threw up my hands and said, "Mercy!"

Holmes smirked. He wasn't too big on mercy, but he would give me a pause. "Take all the time you need," he said. "I owe you a lot of information now, who's up next?"

I pointed to the queen I took from him, and felt a little bit better about my prospects, because my queen was still on the board, and her moves were the most powerful and far-reaching.

"Queen for a queen," I said. "Who do you have for me?"

"Christina of Sweden," Holmes said.

"Goodbye England," I said.

"Indeed," agreed Holmes. "She was thought to be male at birth because she was born hairy, which may have helped set the tenor of her life. Her father King Gustav II Adolf was pleased with this, saying, 'She'll be clever, she has made fools of us all!' She was coronated as a king in 1650, with a Silver Throne made especially for her, which is still used for coronations, accessions to the throne, and other parliamentary pomp. She soon became known as the Minerva of the North throughout Europe. Pope Alexander VII described Christina as 'a queen without a realm, a Christian without faith, and a woman without shame.' This may be due to her overwhelming distaste for marriage. She greatly admired our own Elizabeth I."

"The virgin queen of England, last of the Tudor monarchs," Watson said, before turning to me with more backstory. "She was the ruler who oversaw the execution of Mary, Queen of Scots, and was succeeded by the King James we heard of earlier. She never married."

"Can't say I blame her," I said. "No offense, dear, but if I were a queen, I think I'd have enough to worry about looking after myself, I'd have no incentive to bring a king into the mix."

"You could marry him and keep him powerless," Holmes said. "The spouse of the queen is her consort, he'd have no constitutional standing outside of emotional sway over your heart."

"Perfect!" I said to Watson, grinning. "No children though."

"That was an issue with Christina as well, who in 1649 announced that she would not marry, and instead selected her first cousin Charles Gustav as her heir to the throne. He was coronated the next year as her official successor, leaving Christina with unbothered time for an intimate relationship with her lady-in-waiting, Ebba Sparre, whom she introduced as her 'bed-fellow.'"

"That doesn't sound so bad," I said.

"It wasn't good enough, however," Holmes said, "since Christina abdicated her throne in 1654 amidst popular displeasure at her beheading of a man and his son who'd gone around calling her a Jezebel. She left Sweden disguised in men's clothes, went to Rome, secretly converted to Catholicism, and traveled in exile, with Italy as her new home base. It was in Italy that she died in 1689. The pope had her body placed on display for four days with a gilt crown and scepter, a silver mask, and a virginal white brocade."

"There are worse ways to go," I said. She quit her duties and traveled the world for years, I'd say that's much better than being forced off the throne and executed like so many others.

"They're making a movie about her," Holmes said. "I hear Greta Garbo will play her, which, if what I hear about Garbo is at all true, she's well-suited to play the bachelor queen."

I looked at Watson. We like Greta Garbo. Suddenly we knew that Greta Garbo liked women.

"Who is next?" Watson asked.

I pointed to my fallen knight and said, "Another king?"

"Yes," Holmes said, and got out his pipe and tobacco to have a smoke while he caught up on his chessboard conquests. "Another Swedish monarch, King Charles XII, who took the throne after his father Charles XI, who was the son and successor of Christina's cousin Gustav. Also known as Carolus Rex, Charles XII had a somewhat rougher go of the throne, and life. After his father died of an aggressive abdominal cancer, Carolus Rex ascended to throne at age fifteen."

"Hmm," Watson interjected. Fifteen is such a perilous age.

Holmes went on. "Inexperienced, the young Rex started wars he refused to end peacefully, attacking countries with leaders he perceived as weak. Like Christina before him, he refused to marry and produced no children. Instead he had a particularly close relationship with a volunteer for his army, Maximilian Emanuel of Württemberg-Winnental, whom he said was 'very pretty,' his 'best and truest friend,' his 'Little Prince.' Carolus Rex was shorter-lived than his own father, killed when he was hit by a projectile when inspecting trenches in 1718. He may have been killed by an assassin sent by his brother-in-law, but in the fog of war, no one can say definitively. What is sure is that the throne then passed to his sister, Ulrika Eleonora, who was quickly coerced into surrendering her reign over to her husband, who then became King Frederick I of Sweden."

"He sounds like an awfully presumptuous consort," I said, which made my dear Watson laugh. I am confident the husband I have chosen is not the kind who would usurp me.

"Well, the younger the monarch, the more trouble you're likely to get, as with Mad King Ludwig II of Bavaria," Holmes said, tapping the pawn he claimed from me so I could lay it, too, on its side. We were moving on to the next.

"How old was he?" Watson asked.

"Ludwig took the Bavarian throne at eighteen, and quickly ran the country into debt. His ministers declared him mentally ill—"

"Hence the 'mad' epithet," I interjected.

"—but despite their best efforts he held his throne for over twenty years until his incredibly suspicious death at age forty. They said he drowned, but he was found in the shallows and had no water in his lungs. Perhaps he committed suicide, but what of the bruises on his body, were there marks of strangulation? That all remains a mystery. What was not mysterious, however, was the reason he never married. Ludwig tried to stifle his desire for men with Catholicism, which did not work—"

"Has it ever?" I interrupted again, earning a shrug from Holmes, as religion was forever outside of his interest.

"Though he was once engaged to a Duchess Sophie, it was an intimacy that hinged on a mutual love and appreciation for the work of Richard Wagner."

"What happened to Sophie?" Watson asked.

"What happened is that King Ludwig met Richard Wagner."

"Oh my," I said.

"Wagner was introduced to the newly minted King Ludwig in 1864, when Wagner was fifty-one and Ludwig still eighteen. Wagner found Ludwig to be 'so handsome and wise, soulful and lovely,' and Ludwig felt that Wagner was beyond imagination. He wrote to Wagner saying, 'My enthusiasm and love for you are boundless.' His interest in Wagner revived the composer's career, but Wagner's scandalous personal behavior forced Ludwig to ask him to leave Bavaria by the next year. Ludwig wanted to abdicate his throne and travel with Wagner instead, an urge that Wagner discouraged. Part of the debt King Ludwig amassed was created in settling up Wagner's accounts, funding the completion of Wagner's personal opera house at Bayreuth, and paying for the construction of a villa for Wagner's family."

"It sounds like Wagner needed his admirer to stay a king, with access to the king's coffers," Watson said.

"Most probably," said Holmes. "Ludwig's devotion was known far and wide for what it was, as far as the United States, as seen in 1888 when Charles I of the brief Kingdom of Württemberg in what is now Germany became infatuated with some American travelers, lavishing them with gifts and titles. The newspapers reported that the Americans were 'playing Piers Gaveston parts in Germany' and that the scandal of it all 'reminds one of the late unfortunate Bavarian King Ludwig.'"

"Such infamy," I said. "Does Charles of Württemberg count as my second bishop?" I pointed to the last of the currently conquered chess pieces beside the board.

"Why not?" Holmes said. "There are plenty more pieces left in play."

And yet, no more pieces were captured. Holmes and I danced back and forth until we boxed ourselves into a wonderful circumstance (as far as I'm concerned): a stalemate. It wasn't a win for me, but it wasn't a loss either. I played very well tonight, so well that Holmes could not beat me, he could only match me.

When Watson looked over the board and said, "It looks like we'll have to call this a draw," I clapped as if I had won. Holmes was quick to throw a shadow over my small victory.

"It's a shame the game wasn't more contentious, Mrs. Watson," he said, taking a sketch of the final formation in his notebook for future contemplation before reassembling the pieces back to the starting points on their respective sides. "I had another pair in mind for you, the curious relationship between our own Richard the Lionhearted and King Philip II of France."

"You're kidding," I said, almost hopeful that he was kidding, as that would be preferable to getting teased with information that would lead to yet another match and my likely defeat.

"You mean the two of them...?" Watson began. "With one another, they were...?"

"I wish I could say," Holmes said, "but unless I capture two more pieces from your wife, I'm afraid I can't."

Traitorous consort that he is, my Watson turned to me. "Fancy another game, darling?"

The Traubel With Whitman

December 19th 1932

It looks like we're going to have Holmes for the holidays.

I'm not as upset about this as I would have been a few years ago. When last we met, Holmes and I actually had a couple of decent conversations, so surely it won't be a disaster, but who drops in just before Christmas like this? He's past his days of chasing down capers, what on earth brought him to our neighborhood? He's not really the sentimental type, even during the Yuletide, but I'm not all that precious about it either—Watson's the one who still likes to open presents, if not for him I wouldn't even wrap them.

Holmes showed up this morning while I was still in my robe and slippers, his face bright with pink from traveling through a snowy day. That's lovely circulation for a man of seventy-eight. Watson answered the door and practically squealed to see Holmes, or maybe that sound came when Holmes grabbed Watson's face with his long, chilly fingers to give him a kiss. I couldn't see from where I sat near the fire, but I certainly knew there was only one person in the world who would make Watson so happy, and it wasn't the mailman.

"Darling, you'll never believe who's here," Watson said as he returned. Without looking up from my book, I greeted our guest.

"Hello, Mr. Holmes."

"Mrs. Watson," he acknowledged in response, while Watson became even more overjoyed wondering how I knew. Holmes and I smirked at each other, a good start to another odd visit. It's not so hard to be a wizard of deduction, provided you know your audience.

"I suppose you'd like some tea," I said to Holmes, before holding out my cup to Watson. "For us both, dear?"

Watson happily complied, and Holmes joined me at the fireside.

"You're looking well, madam," Holmes told me, crossing his legs knee-over-knee and smoothing his trousers. I did not look well, which is what he meant to imply, I looked like I'd been sleeping in a heap of dirty laundry, but I did not take his bait.

"Say, Holmes, you spent time in America... where do you like Christmas better, here or there?" That was me trying to be gracious and inviting, as is the want of my sex or so I hear, but a fat lot of good it did.

"I don't like Christmas anywhere," he said. "I rather think most everyone misses the spirit of the holiday, but if they buy the trappings it's as if they've done something good and charitable."

"What do you think about Lent then? May I guess? Do you believe that forty days of unnecessary sobriety or self-control are not enough, that it's just an invitation for gluttons to be tourists of asceticism?"

"And then pat themselves on the back as if they've cleansed their sins, yes. I know many a murderer who would love it if the justice system worked that way, forty days in prison for every murder, theft, or malicious injury."

"Sounds like the makings for a pretty lawless world," I told him.

"Well, they say that about the American West too, but it isn't so bad as that, though I spent my time closer to the east coast, in the cities."

"Which cities?" Somehow I knew I wouldn't have to remind Holmes I was educated in New England, one place as a child, another as a teenager, and a third spot as a governess of sorts to let me learn about hearth and home, I imagine (it didn't really take—I enjoy sitting beside a hearth but know very little about how to operate one). I have read Watson's recounts of Holmes in America, but it was years ago, and Watson's details were skimpy too, as he and Holmes were separated for a while before the Great War. Watson was more focused on me in those days.

"Chicago and Buffalo, mostly, though I did a bit of urban exploring."

"Any of it fit to tell a lady?" I asked him, which is about when Watson reappeared with three tea cups and some sandwiches on a very precarious tray. Holmes reached his long, iron grip out to take the tray single-handedly from Watson and deposit it on an ottoman between he and I. Watson scooted up a third chair, and joined us.

"What are you two talking about?"

"America," I told him.

"Oh, lovely. You've both been there, you know, you should have that in common too."

Watson is under the impression that Holmes and I have more in common than our affection for him, and likes to point that out: 'Oh, I say, you can both read! You're both so interested in breathing day and night, and yet neither one of you enjoys having a cold, uncanny!' I'm exaggerating, but hardly.

"Your wife is asking me if I have any stories from there that I might repeat without ruining the holiday spirit, and you know, I think I have, considering some of our previous conversations. Would the lady be interested in some gossip?"

As if to defend women's equality, Watson chimed in quickly with, "Holmes, you know we'd both enjoy that."

My dear Watson is my knight in even the smallest of ways. My smile deepened and Holmes rolled his eyes, but stayed a good sport about it.

"Right, well then: what do you know of Walt Whitman?"

"*Leaves of Grass*," I said instantly, as if I were answering a teacher in school. "You know I wasn't able to get near a copy of that book until I was good and well an adult back in England, it had such a reputation and I was always policed by minders in America."

Holmes nodded, knowing that all of what I said was true. "I was able to see a very early edition of it in someone's very private collection once, it's more American than it is obscene, because that's just the way Americans are."

I couldn't argue with him there, I found Americans to be terribly open and honest; they taught me loud habits I still have to this day.

"Well, most of what anyone knows these days about Walt Whitman is known because he too had a Watson of sorts," and with that Holmes reached to squeeze my husband's arm for a moment. "A Mr. Horace Traubel, a biographer extraordinaire."

"Now that name I do know," Watson said. "Mr. Traubel was bringing out volume after volume of information on Whitman, his letters, his conversations, his habits and home."

"Exhaustive," I said, because it was in two senses: thorough to the point of depletion, and of course it all sounds exhausting to try to read.

Holmes nodded and continued. "He put out several volumes before he died, but the work is still not complete. I'm sure they'll get it all out eventually, but no one has the same fervor for it that Horace did. I haven't read any of those archives because the peculiarities of a dead poet would have no use for me, but I did hear a few things from Mr. Traubel when I met him. He seemed to talk more about Whitman than he did about himself."

Dear diary, I know the type. I hear more about Sherlock Holmes than I do about the weather, what's for dinner, and the goings-on of our royalty combined.

"Did you go to New Jersey then?" I asked. "It was *With Walt Whitman in Camden*, was it not?"

"It was, but I did not. I met Horace in New York, where he would hold an annual Walt Whitman fellowship meeting, as if the man had been a prophet, and Horace a convert who wanted to spread the gospel of 'comradeship.' But of course, in the spirit of the original intent, it wasn't only meant to deify one man. Horace said to those gathered, 'I've been wondering how it would be if sometime we'd come here and

celebrate ourselves for a change and not even mention Walt's name!'
It was a very agrarian sort of meeting."

"What made you go there in the first place?" I asked, though I already
knew the answer: to find said 'comradeship,' most likely.

"I was in America to infiltrate its seedy underbelly, and you must
know that when it comes to my work," a slight shrug here, "I cover
the waterfront."

I have no idea where he picked up that phrase, but I do understand
it. It's seedy-sounding indeed, like trolling along the docks looking
for trouble.

"I was there under my assumed identity, the Irish-American Mr.
Altamont, but I wasn't the oddest one in attendance. There was
something about The Good Gray Poet that made him a man of just
about any people, from communists to anarchists, from mystics to
pacifists, those in favor of free love and women's rights, those in
the labor movement. I happened to meet a very close friend of Mr.
Traubel's there, Frank Bain, the husband of Mildred Bain, who had
just that year written a biography of Horace himself. Horace was an
intimate friend of the whole family, you see, so intimate that their
children were biologically Horace's children."

I wanted to contradict him, say there was no way he could be sure of
that unless he was told, but in the moment I thought it, I remembered
how he solved that whole Baskerville Hall demon hound situation, by
seeing facial features in a portrait and knowing who was that man's
true kin.

"The husband didn't mind?" I asked. As pleasant and breezy as if I
was offering him a scone.

"How could he begrudge her relationship with Horace if she didn't
begrudge his? Within a year of meeting Horace, the Bains were as
much 'Traubelites' as Whitmanites."

"Or Whitmaniacs, as the press like to phrase it," Watson volunteered.
Holmes nodded before continuing.

"Indeed, Horace was the closest man to true mania I've ever met who never fully succumbed to madness. He had the energy of a zealot, but because he felt his efforts had purpose, served a higher calling, he never tired of pursuing them. More books produced meant more converts, more converts meant a farther-reaching message, and the wider the message, the more immortal the name of Whitman. Horace met Whitman as a teenager, when the old man was half-paralyzed by a stroke. Whitman moved in with his younger brother, George Washington Whitman, for care and stability, and young Horace was suddenly his new neighbor. They struck up a friendship that caused quite a scandal. Whitman had a filthy reputation, the author of sex poems about robust and amorous men, and there he was going on long walks with a young boy and talking about books? Which books? How dare he? The neighbors told Horace's mother not to let her son associate with the 'lecherous old man,' but that of course is the fastest way to inspire true devotion in a young man. You'll recall, Watson, that you once warned our page Billy away from my influence? He still writes to me, asks for my advice, basks in my praise. It's a deeper attachment than many sons have for their fathers."

"Healthy boys need to reject their fathers, or at least their father's failings," I chimed in. I had enough brothers to know how most men behave. "That relationship is always a little fraught, but the man they can choose, the man they admire whose attention they feel they've *earned*? That devotion could easily last a lifetime."

Of course with Billy, it's more likely he's still so fond of Holmes because of their sexual relationship, but I didn't bring up that part of it; if Holmes wasn't that boy's first love, he was certainly his first affair, and no one ever forgets that.

"That is about what Horace felt for Walt Whitman, if not more so, with the spiritual aspect thrown in. Tell me, Mrs. Watson, what do women do with the men they admire and *earn* affection from? Are those the men they marry?"

"Not as far as I've seen," I told him. "Women marry the men who admire them, if they're smart."

Perhaps I was speaking of myself, for that is what I did. Certainly the friends I have who married during the honeymoon of youthful devotion don't have that same relationship anymore. I suspect it's a matter of maturity: men can stay boys forever, but all girls become women, the world insists.

"Did Mr. Traubel know who he was talking to?" Watson asked. "Or did you stay in character the whole time?"

"He never knew I was Sherlock Holmes, no. I couldn't let anyone know that, but when you talked to Horace, you didn't have much of an opportunity to talk about yourself, or about himself, for that matter—the more pressing topic was always Walt Whitman. He asked me as Mr. Altamont where I was from, but only so he could tell me that Whitman hated how America often replaced the native names of the New World with titles from Old Europe. The uninspired *Long Island* instead of *Paumanok*, *Washington* instead of *Tacoma*, *West Virginia* over *Kanawtha*, and *New York City* after the regrettable Duke of York in place of his preferred and beloved *Mannahatta*."

"I agree with Mr. Whitman on that," I said. "Berlin, New Hampshire doesn't remind one of Berlin or Hampshire."

Holmes nodded. "All of New England is like no England I'd ever seen, but perhaps those names were chosen out of some sense of colonial rebellion, a bit of leftover spite after those tea taxes they so disagreed with. 'Welcome to Paris, it's in the desert; this is our Cambridge, we've put it in a tundra; come to one of our many New Londons, we have heaps of them, as common as vermin.'"

Watson snorted with laughter, and I smiled too. If only the Americans were that darkly comic, but most of the ones I met led me to believe they simply couldn't think up enough new names.

"Horace himself had loosely tossed white hair, and bright blue eyes that were both boyish and strangely wise, like the eyes of a young clairvoyant. He had a short mustache, came from a German Jewish father and Christian mother, and cheerfully called himself a 'half-breed.' He was married, and had a daughter and son with his wife, though by the time I met him, his son had died of scarlet fever. As devastating as that must have been, he was never disconsolate, but rather unceasingly dynamic, as his biographer Mrs. Bain phrased it. While Whitman was 'a philosopher, a mystic, a dreamer... big, slow-moving, phlegmatic,' she described Traubel as, while also a philosopher, a 'direct, child-like, and vital' one. I think she got it quite correct."

I raised my eyebrows, as it's not often that Holmes so unreservedly gives a woman credit, but it was nice to hear.

"So where is the gossip?" Watson asked then.

"Oh, right, well maybe after lunch if you don't mind. I'm afraid I neglected to eat breakfast."

And that was that for this morning. Someone's picked up some storytelling skills from our dear Watson—he left us hanging, and anxious for more.

December 20th 1932

We found out yesterday afternoon why Holmes has decided to grace us with his presence. It's not some sentimental holiday spirit, it's because he has business in London pretty soon, and our home is closer to London than his, and there's a ferocious snowstorm he swears will make its way through just before he needs to be there, and he'd rather cover the distance before the snowfall than through it. Quite practical, I'm sure, though I wonder how he knows there's a storm coming. I don't doubt his prediction, I just wonder what kind of contraption he has that lets him know the changes of the wind so well, some kind of windmill made out of spoons or something? Something that would have looked like witchcraft a century ago, perhaps? Oh well; I want to know, but I don't want to ask. C'est la vie.

We didn't manage to get back on the topic of Walt Whitman even after dinner, so I graciously retired to the library to let the boys have some time to themselves. I was interested in locating the copy of Leaves of Grass I knew I'd seen around there somewhere, but it turned out it was in Watson's office, from whence I retrieved it back to the library. While I was on that trip I overheard the men talking. Just a few innocuous words about the worst snowstorms they each remembered, which in the next sentence I'm sure led them to the topic of snowstorms they shared in Baker Street; that is the part I leave alone.

Anyway, I will confess I was looking through *Leaves of Grass* out of a purely prurient interest, because I didn't remember them well at all: just how scandalous and sexual could these verses be? I say 'verses' but they aren't the type we were taught in school, the sort that rhyme, with the exact right amount of syllables. Whitman's 'poems' are lists and ramblings and philosophies and seem messy to me, that is they did before I read a few pages and allowed myself to become hypnotized. I stopped looking for the ends of sentences before I even started them, and after that it was like allowing a river's current to take you around its every bend. His work is full of nature, he's even got me talking in rivers now, but that's not so bad. Whitman was right that America in particular was wild and overgrown with nature, and he clearly loved it that way.

He loved a lot of other things too, himself, and men, and sex, possibly in that order, it all sort of swirls together. For example, in his "Song of Myself," he clearly intends to celebrate himself from top to bottom, but in section five there is also this pearl-clutching passage:

> *Loafe with me on the grass, loose the stop from your throat,*
> *Not words, not music or rhyme I want, not custom or lecture,*
> *not even the best,*
> *Only the lull I like, the hum of your valvèd voice.*
> *I mind how once we lay such a transparent summer morning,*
> *How you settled your head athwart my hips and gently*
> *turn'd over upon me,*
> *And parted the shirt from my bosom-bone, and plunged*
> *your tongue to my bare-stript heart,*
> *And reach'd till you felt my beard, and reach'd till you held*
> *my feet.*

That is quite a visual: what would rest between Whitman's feet and his beard that one could put their tongue on? His 'bare-stript heart' of course, which is one of the better phrases I've heard for the thing. A few passages later in section twenty-two, he talks rather frankly of the sea:

> *You sea! I resign myself to you also—I guess what you mean,*
> *I behold from the beach your crooked inviting fingers,*
> *I believe you refuse to go back without feeling of me,*
> *We must have a turn together, I undress, hurry me out of*
> *   sight of the land,*
> *Cushion me soft, rock me in billowy drowse,*
> *Dash me with amorous wet, I can repay you.*

That is *quite* some love for the ocean, so much so that I think I'm safe in assuming there's more to what he's saying than what is explicitly written. Just after that passage it's all 'ground-swells' and 'convulsive breaths,' and by the end of over fifty sections just like it, I was so bewildered and bothered that Watson was able to see it on my face when he came to fetch me for bed. He fell asleep that night reading the same long prose-poem I had just completed, and I went to bed with wild dreams of leaves, and tendrils, and bodies of water, literally: bodies made of water and crashing into one another with foamy, ecstatic spray. Watson and I both woke up with questions and curiosities, and at some point today we mean to get them answered.

December 21st 1932

Well, well, did we ever get an earful last night.

Holmes was so pleased to see us both come looking for more stories that an incredibly self-satisfied grin came across his face. He sat down in our comfiest chair like a king before his groveling subjects, and Watson and I went to him, each of us at one of his knees, to be regaled.

"So where was I? Ah yes, with Mr. Horace Traubel. Eventually the other members of his little fellowship gathering went home, and he and I were left alone to stay up late. The man is without limit when he's talking of Whitman, which is apparently something he learned from Whitman himself. For such a filthy, hairy, only occasionally employed loaf, Walt Whitman thought very highly of himself, as did their assassinated leader, President Lincoln."

"Really? When did Lincoln meet him? I knew Whitman wrote some elegies for the president after his death, but..." Watson began, just as I was saying, "He surely does like himself. The poem I read last night for instance, I wanted to bring it up because..."

Holmes waved his long, thin hands back and forth to silence us. Watson and I obeyed like well-behaved school children.

"One at a time," he said. "Whitman received a letter from someone who was speaking with the president when Whitman just happened to be sauntering by across the street from the White House. He crossed before the gaze of Mr. Lincoln, quite slow, 'with hands in the breastpockets of his overcoat, wearing a sizeable felt hat on his head pretty well up,' which distracted the president. Once he was out of sight, Mr. Lincoln asked who that was, and was answered, and then said very emphatically, 'Well, *he* looks like a *man*.' Then it was back to the task at hand." Holmes took a sip of tea at this moment before continuing. "It might also be interesting for you both to know that only one woman is confirmed to have shared Mr. Lincoln's bed, that being his wife Mary Todd, but there were several men. His close friend Joshua Speed before his marriage, they shared a bed for four years, and even after moving to the White House, his bodyguard Captain Derickson was invited to sleep with him when Mrs. Lincoln was away. They enjoyed an intimacy so deep that Derickson was welcome to make use of 'his excellency's nightshirt,' at least that's what was published by someone after the war, writing a history of one of their regiments. They seemed to think nothing of it, perhaps it was innocent. Perhaps Mr. Lincoln was only poor before his marriage, and then terribly cold without a bedmate for the rest of his life. He was a very thin man."

"He could have gotten a dog," Watson suggested.

"Or a bed warmer," I said. "He was the president, I'm sure someone would have obliged."

"Hmm," Holmes said, gazing benevolently at both me and Watson (have I become part of their 'family' at last?), before concluding that part of his tale with, "Lincoln seemed to prefer men to be his bed warmers."

I opened my mouth to ask about my question, but Holmes nodded at me before I could speak and began to answer it.

"As to Whitman's almost charming vanity, not only did he once anonymously publish a glowing review of himself, and not only did he take it upon himself to quote a letter from Emerson on the very cover of his book without asking, which nearly ended their association, but Horace told me a much smaller detail on the night we talked. Whitman thought the world of himself and was unashamed about it, which might be his most appealing attribute, that earnest shamelessness. A man once asked him, 'Don't you feel rather sorry on the whole that you wrote the sex poems?' and Whitman answered him by asking another question: 'Don't you feel rather sorry on the whole that I am Walt Whitman?'"

"Marvelous," Watson murmured.

I thought so too. What a remarkable gift, to be able to love and admire one's own self that much, especially if he was as it seems, a man who loved men. Not everyone is as confident he is right and pure as Mr. Whitman, not even Sherlock Holmes. Certainly Holmes knows that he's right more often than not, but pure, kind, loveable? I'm sure he has his struggles too, as our dear Watson does sometimes with shame and disgust. He wanted to be a happily married man, but he is not always that, because of his feelings for Holmes. I wonder if Watson ever feels rather sorry on the whole that he met Sherlock Holmes.

"I don't think I got as far as the 'sex poems,'" I volunteered then. "I'll have to keep reading."

"Indeed," said Holmes. "Whitman was never once sorry for those, not even when they got him fired."

"Who fired him?" Watson asked.

"He was working as a clerk in the Department of the Interior in Washington D.C., and the Secretary of the Interior, a Mr. James Harlan, took it upon himself to go through Whitman's papers. He found Whtiman's marked-up copy of *Leaves of Grass* (as he was always revising it for the next edition), read it, became offended by it, and then quickly fired its author."

"Outrageous," I huffed, while Watson shook his head in disapproval.

"He hadn't broken any rules, wasn't wasting time at work, he wasn't sub-par in any of his duties, nothing?" Watson asked.

"He was asked about that specifically by someone who went to confront Harlan over the dismissal. He asked why Whitman was dismissed, whether he had been found inattentive to his duties or incompetent for them, but Harlan did not retreat. Harlan said Walt Whitman was perfectly competent, but he was also the author of *Leaves of Grass*, and that this author was a 'free lover' and so unfit to work there. Even after being told of the good Whitman had done, of the esteem he had from honorable men of all sorts, Mr. Harlan held firm and said, 'I will not have the man who wrote *Leaves of Grass* in this Department. If the President himself were to order his reinstatement, I would resign myself sooner than put him back.' Whitman's friends secured him a position in the Attorney General's office instead. It wasn't right, but it wasn't going to be rectified, and that was that."

Watson and I tsked and harrumphed after hearing that, while Holmes fetched a piece of paper and a pencil out of his pocket and started to sketch something.

"It was a public defense of Whitman over that firing which earned him the name The Good Gray Poet, so something good came from it," Holmes said, before showing us his piece of paper and asking us, "What do these look like to you?"

They looked like a dirty drawing, like little spermatozoa wriggling around on the page. Watson clearly saw what I saw too, and looked at me wondering what strange turn this presentation had taken.

Holmes smirked, and tucked his notebook back into his pocket. "I'm in my right to tell you both to get your minds out of the gutter, those were sprouting seedlings, what else could they have been? Nothing but leaves about to shoot through warm soil towards the sun. One of Whitman's editions of *Leaves of Grass* has those 'seeds' swimming around the title page. Thus, I'm sure he couldn't have been too surprised to have someone take offense and punish him for his brazenness. As Mr. Oscar Wilde once wrote, and had quoted maliciously back at him in court, 'If one tells the truth, one is sure, sooner or later, to be found out.' Wilde met Whitman once, shall I tell that story too?"

"In just a moment," I said, before springing up to fetch our copy of *Leaves*. I brought it back to the sitting room forthwith and opened it to the title page, and lo and behold: it was *true*. Depending on how close your mind was to 'the gutter' as Holmes phrased it, there were seeds either growing from or struggling to impregnate the word GRASS on the title page. I looked at Watson and found the same look of delighted wonder on his face as I felt on mine—to think this had been in our house for years, and we never noticed. It was like finding an Easter egg on Christmas.

After a hushed moment of silence, Holmes went on.

"When Oscar Wilde visited America, he was twenty-seven years old. There were some amusing anecdotes there, for instance that his Oxford accent deceived some miners in Colorado into thinking they could out-drink him, not realizing they were challenging an Irishman. Also his commentary on Niagara Falls being a disappointment, and his sympathy for every bride who is taken there on her honeymoon; he said that 'the sight of the stupendous waterfall must be one of the earliest, if not the keenest, disappointments in American married life.'"

I let out a very unladylike snort of laughter there—cheers, Mr. Wilde! I wondered how Niagara compared to Reichenbach, but I didn't ask, and Holmes continued.

"Whitman was an old man by then, in his sixties and living in Camden. Wilde wanted to meet him, and his publisher was gracious enough to set them up together and leave them alone for a couple of hours. When Wilde gave an interview about their meeting, he was quite effusive, saying Whitman was 'the grandest man' he had ever seen, 'the simplest, most natural, strongest character,' that he was 'wonderful, large, entire.' Whitman produced some homemade elderberry wine, which one would think too crude for even a young Wilde, though when he was asked how he managed to tolerate such fare, Wilde replied, 'If it had been vinegar I would have drunk it all the same, for I have an admiration for that man which I can hardly express.'"

"How sweet," Watson said. I smiled at him, for Watson himself is that sweet, it's why I married him. Perhaps Constance Wilde knew that same feeling once.

Holmes nodded. "Apparently they were very quickly on 'thee and thou terms,' Whitman's phrase, and he later characterized Wilde as 'a fine large handsome youngster' with 'the good sense to take a great fancy to me.' I have it on good authority that Wilde ultimately wrote to a friend revealing, 'I have the kiss of Walt Whitman still on my lips.' There's some gossip for you, if you'd like to speculate. He wasn't the only one to make that sort of pilgrimage to meet Whitman, Bram Stoker did as well, for about the same reasons, though with much less theatrical flair."

"The same reasons as in... but didn't Stoker marry Oscar Wilde's old childhood sweetheart?" I asked.

"Certainly, but then again I find that people marry for all sorts of strange reasons."

At that, Holmes looked at his watch and declared he was growing tired of the sound of his own voice, and that he would impart more information tomorrow. That was fine with Watson and I, for we certainly *do* want some time to speculate on the Whitman and Wilde suggestion. First, however, there's the matter of meals, and most probably another evening apart, with the men left to the company of one another, and me already anxious to pore over *Leaves of Grass* looking for something I can recommend to Watson by the time we reunite for bed. Must get to it!

December 23rd 1932

Where shall I begin now?

Well, first of all, the night of the 21st was fascinating. By the time Watson and I were alone again, he had picked up even more privileged information from Holmes that he was quite excited to share with me as soon as possible. He'll have to read the poems I marked out for him later, because we talked ourselves to sleep that night, and would have kept going irresponsibly if we didn't know better by now how miserable a bad night's sleep can make the following day at our respective ages.

Watson's information began with him finding out just how intimate the conversation between Traubel and Holmes as the Irish Altamont had gotten: they ultimately found themselves discussing Whitman's boys, his men, and his tastes concerning them. Whitman kept lists apparently, very diligent and detailed lists about the men he met walking the streets day and night, their professions (they were all rough, working men), their appearances, and how much time they spent together. Sometimes they only talked for the length of an omnibus ride, sometimes they 'slept together,' and apparently the greatest of these was a young man named Peter Doyle, a streetcar conductor who met Whitman on a stormy night.

Watson relayed it to me like this: "The way Holmes told it, even he couldn't stop it from sounding romantic. When Peter later recalled their first encounter, he said he saw Walt with a blanket thrown around his shoulders, like an old sea-captain in the rain. Peter was the conductor of the streetcar, and Walt was the only passenger on a lonely night, and they were both inexplicably drawn to one another. He said, 'We were familiar at once—I put my hand on his knee—we understood.' Isn't that amazing?"

It was amazing to me that Watson was already on a first-name basis with this Doyle, when I as his wife am still not on a first-name basis with him, as I just don't see the point. Our intimacy is of an entirely different sort and always has been, clearly.

"Holmes and Traubel—Horace—do you think that they...?" I asked.

"I'd certainly bet on it," Watson whispered. We were getting into bed, shivering in the semi-darkness of a bright moon (I guess that snowstorm Holmes told us about was far closer to his part of the country than ours), and then nestled together, heads close for our strange sort of 'pillow talk.' "I doubt Holmes went to a Whitman fellowship meeting because he wanted to go home alone," Watson continued, "and he speaks very familiarly of Traubel."

"His boyish spirit," I whispered back. "It's the same thing he likes about you."

"Hmm, perhaps so," responded Watson. We've both grown quite comfortable as the years have gone by with speaking plainly. "I was actually thinking that he had more in common with Whitman as far as his preferences, working men."

"Well, it sounds to me that Whitman liked extremely working-class men, as in men who can't even read, whereas Holmes will take to any working man from the boys at the docks to office professionals, so long as they do *something*, and they do it honestly. Your stories of him show little patience for the landed, the lazy, those rich off of something other than their own labors, be they mental or physical."

"True, true, there's your woman's intuition, dear," he said, leaning over to kiss my cheek.

I kissed him back and said, "It's observation, my dear Watson. I once taught it in elementary school."

That got us both laughing, giggling really. We talked late into the night about men of all sorts, and most particularly my theory that nothing more intimate than talk and gossip passed between Whitman and Wilde, as Oscar Wilde was no working-class man, and Walt Whitman was no gilded-lily youth. More likely if they were delighted in meeting each other, it was more as long-lost father and son. What they had in common would have prided them each greatly—their largess, their boldness, their fervor to bring love and art and beauty to a new age—and their differences in preference would have amused them. After all... there's no accounting for taste.

Watson and I speculated until we were dry in the mouths, and before I fell asleep I thought, 'How strange it is that the sudden appearance of Holmes at our door has brought us more joy than a Christmas alone and undisturbed would have done?' It didn't use to be that way, but somehow we've gotten here.

Yesterday, however, Holmes announced that he would be leaving today.

"My appointment in London is on Christmas Day, so I must leave first thing tomorrow morning. I thank you for sparing me the storm by harboring me here."

Watson and I said 'of course, of course, any time,' but we were both a little disappointed. There was so much we knew we hadn't heard, after all, like what about Bram Stoker and Whitman? But that will have to be a story for another day, apparently, as yesterday Holmes was compelled to tell us everyone's endings.

"Whitman died in 1892, at seventy-two. His health had never been the same after his stroke in 1873, which he attributed to 'hospital malaria' he caught while volunteering in America's Civil War hospitals. Doyle was present at his funeral, which Horace and another close friend and biographer of Whitman's worried he might not be, for after eight years of grand friendship, of being 'the biggest sort of friends' according to Doyle, they grew apart after Whitman's stroke caused him to move to Camden, where he met Horace Traubel. Though he came later to Whitman's life, Horace thought it would have been sad that for all the people who knew Whitman, or knew of him, and came to pay their respects, what if the one man missing was to be the 'son of responding kisses' Whitman treasured so dearly? But he was there, Horace made note of it as he did everything in Whitman's life. He spotted Doyle 'twirling a switch in his hand, his tall figure and big soft hat impressively set against the white-blue sky,' and called him over to speak. Apparently Doyle seemed 'immobile, not greatly moved by the occasion, yet was sincere and simple and expressed in his demeanor the powers by which he must have attracted Walt.'"

"Well that's something," my Watson said. Something more than nothing, which is all you can hope for sometimes.

"Horace and his wife stayed friends with Doyle, and Horace continued publishing essays and his volumes of recordings to promote Whitman, but life caught up to each of them. Doyle died of a kidney disease at sixty-three. Horace suffered the loss of his own son to scarlet fever before I met him, and he was trampled by a horse in 1909, which did some lasting damage. He was still as energetic as he could be in 1913 when we shared an evening together, but he never knew who I truly was, and the next year his health became worse, his heart in particular. He lived long enough to see his daughter have a grandson, and to see the one-hundred-year anniversary of Whitman's birthday on May 31st of 1919. He attended a celebration of that day in New York, but by August he wrote that he was seeing visions of Whitman beckoning him into the beyond, and by September 3rd he was dead at sixty-one."

With all the fun we'd had hearing about people's grand and flagrant youths, their jolly and robust adult years, I thought we had to resign ourselves to Holmes leaving us this *memento mori* under our tree, this reminder that we too are old and waning. Even I, the youngest by many years of the three of us, will turn sixty next year. Is this all borrowed time from now on? Have our lives already been lived, and every tomorrow we still possess is a day we'll spend waiting for death?

December 24th, 1932

I assumed that would be all from Holmes, that we'd had our fun, that maybe it was indeed best he moved on so Watson and I would have time to recover some Christmas cheer before opening our presents. I thought that until this morning, when Holmes was dressed to depart, waiting for our driver to take him to the train station.

Looking at his watch, Holmes said, "There's just enough time for one last detail, something rather appropriate for the holiday season."

"What is it?" Watson asked. We were standing at the door waiting to shake hands and kiss goodbye, and with his other hand on the doorknob, Holmes paused to speak.

"I told you Whitman volunteered at the hospitals of that ghastly Civil War they had. Peter Doyle had been a Rebel soldier for a time, though when he left the service he signed a pledge of loyalty to the Union side to get back to his family north of the divide; he had no loyalty further than what could earn him a living. At any rate, it isn't surprising that Whitman was so charmed by him, for he loved taking care of the soldiers. Like his notes of men he met in the streets, he also would go around the hospitals and make notes of what each soldier desired most: an apple, a jar of pickles, a stamp or sheet of paper so as to write a letter home, a bit of whiskey. Whitman lived frugally, saving his own money so he could buy these items for the boys, and in truest thanks, their faces would alight at the sight of him. One man who survived his stay in the hospital said, 'Walt Whitman didn't bring any tracts or Bibles; he didn't ask if you loved the Lord, and didn't seem to care whether you did or not', but rather, 'this old heathen came and gave me a pipe and tobacco... about the most joyous moment of my life.' Another man, Whitman's friend, went with him once, and later recorded that when Whitman took his leave after these visits, voices would call out from the beds pleading 'Walt, Walt, come again!' and asking for farewell kisses, which he happily bestowed."

"That's beautiful," I said, dabbing just a tad less at the corner of my eye than Watson was dabbing at his.

"I'm not even at the best part," Holmes said with a sly smile. "I also said Whitman attributed his later ill-health to spending so much time in these hospitals, but he never regretted it. He told Horace, 'I had to give up health for it—my body—the vitality of my physical self... I never weighed what I gave for what I got but I am satisfied with what I got. What did I get? Well—I got the boys, for one thing: the boys: thousands of them: they were, they are, they will be mine.'"

Holmes paused for dramatic effect, glanced briefly at each of us with those scrutinizing eyes, and then went back to looking casually at his watch before delivering the final blow.

"The image I'd like to leave you with is this: when Whitman did this work as 'a Soldiers' Missionary,' or so he called himself, he was heavily bearded, and every day wore a cheap, wine-colored suit he tucked into large, leather boots. He also carried with him a great haversack full of these gifts and favors to dole out. Now... who does that description remind you of?"

"He was like Santa," Watson said, his voice hushed and his eyes misty. Of course Watson answered him, because I couldn't speak at all lest I burst into womanly tears and interrupt the moment.

"That's the car," Holmes said after that, snapping closed his watch and kissing us each on the cheek, my right and Watson's left, like a ball bouncing between paddles. A kiss for *me*, that was a new development, though it didn't startle me after so pleasant a visit. "Happy Christmas," he said, and then he was out the door and into the freezing wind, leaving Watson and I scrambling to recover in his wake.

Hell-Home

October 2nd 1934

I write this in the wee, early hours of the morning, as our new cat has awoken me and only me for her breakfast. Watson sleeps too soundly, and the little critter tends to step on my hair because it gets her an immediate response. I looked it up in our dictionary, she's like this because cats are twilight creatures, or 'crepuscular' if you must have the rather unpleasant Latin-esque term for it. She's most active at dawn and dusk, unlike humans who are most active at cocktail parties. She's lucky she's so otherwise adorable, sitting atop the desk with me now like a witch's familiar, lazily undulating her tail. To think we found such a regal creature bedraggled at our door in the freezing rain so recently, and now here she is, Mistress of the Manor. That is why we've started calling her Miss Tress, by the way.

Due to some vandalism last year, the neighborhood has decided that for Halloween it would be better for the community to host an event rather than let the children roam loose on Mischief Night and the main event, All Hallows' Eve. It'll be a costume party for the adults, mostly to encourage chaperone turn-out I believe. Watson and

I will be in attendance, a show of support for those among us with human critters under their feet, and we'll even be bringing a guest!

For at last: the time has come, and Sherlock Holmes will visit us again. I never thought I'd be looking forward to seeing the man, but he left us nearly two years ago with secret information teased and untold about Bram Stoker, and a visit in October will most certainly bring it out of him. I shall start re-reading *Dracula* today to prepare for his arrival and to get into a morbid mood. I may even end up with a list of questions, if not at least some ideas for costumes.

October 7th 1934

I must say, if Holmes has stories about Mr. Stoker being a 'man's man' as one might call it, I will indeed have questions, as the women in *Dracula* are terribly attached to one another; I would say suspiciously so. Mina and Lucy came on strong with their friendship: "I am longing to be with you, and by the sea, where we can talk together freely and build our castles in the air." That was Mina to Lucy and in response, "Mina, we have told all our secrets to each other since we were *children*; we have slept together and eaten together, and laughed and cried together; and now, though I have spoken, I would like to speak more." What true love and devotion those girls had for each other; no wonder Mina was so prepared to confront a big icky human-shaped leech, the vampire Count Dracula. With all the husbands and potential husbands around—the book is practically lousy with suitors—it was Mina who had the psychic connection that brought the whole long thing to a close. I found my feminism unexpectedly pleased by those parts of the story, it made up enough for the overly sensual vampire succubus women, to be sure.

Speaking of those women however, my friends and I will be going to this party as a trio of vampire succubi (it's too easy a costume choice, just a low bodice and some bite marks, a pair of fangs). I even suggested a name for the event from the book and others agreed: we'll be calling it 'Hell-Home', based on a line that Van Helsing speaks explaining where their monster can find his infernal rest: "his earth-home, his coffin-home, his hell-home." It should be a good working theme for a haunted house type of *fête*: some fake blood, some fun scares, and everyone home by midnight. With Halloween falling on a Wednesday this year, the party will be held on the Saturday before, the 27th.

Whether or not Holmes will arrive in time for it is yet to be seen; he announced he would come in October, and that was as specific as he got. I'd be curious to know what costume Holmes would put together for such a shindig. Watson has decided he will dress up as President Roosevelt because he wants to wear a stuffed and mounted moose head as the crown jewel of his costume—he'll strap it to his back like a knapsack. If only she were more social he could carry around Miss Tress as his conquered jungle cat, but to be honest, I did not marry a hunter of any sort. I married a healer, and I fear even our domestic cat would best Watson in a fight. Not that he is weak *per se*, but because she is vicious, and like a vampiress would go straight for the jugular as her first strike.

October 8th 1934

Tonight was our first, full-court committee meeting about this hell-party, and I am sorry to report, there is some devilry afoot in our neighborhood. A Christian busy-body sort of devilry, as one of the wives has enlisted her pastor and insists the 'Hell-Home' I suggested should be literally that: a portrayal of the tortures of Hell that we'll all be doomed to if we don't live as Mrs. Ethel Anderson believes we should. The woman has four children, and if my beliefs didn't include a firm assurance that one's first family is an endurance test that will be rewarded if one emerges from it with good character, then I would pity them greatly.

I've tried to limit my interaction with this woman since Watson and I first moved here after the war, I've always found her too pushy. When Ethel helps you it is with the back of her hand: if she gives you a recipe it's because she's 'concerned' that you're losing your figure and need her help to watch your calories; if she compliments your home it's because she's surprised that you could do so much with so little; if she comes to your party for the ancient Celtic festival of the dead, she comes with the only zombie she likes, the risen Jesus Christ. It doesn't help that every time I hear her name I think of the ethyls in chemistry class either.

We'll be meeting again at the end of the week with ideas on ghoulish features the 'Hell-Home' should include, and I fear I might make a few enemies if I have to disagree too strenuously with their propaganda. I'm still in a rather sour mood about the very idea of it, but I should really take Watson's counsel here: I may be building dreadful castles in my mind, with no real problem at all. We discussed some worst-case scenarios over dinner, which ideas I could live with and which I could not. Would a message of temperance be acceptable? Yes. Even Bram Stoker's first book was a temperance novel, rather too pedantic for me to do more than skim, but one must write to one's intended audience, and certainly Mrs. Ethel Anderson wouldn't want anything too creative in her messaging; creativity is where the Devil finds footholds I'm sure. Would a message of chastity be acceptable? Possibly yes, but if the hellish feature of the story is that a woman once 'sullied' will never be pure again, I would have to argue against it. What will I be offering to the committee myself as an alternative? Well, *there's* a better way to spend my time indeed. My dear Watson has advised me well.

I am thinking an entry-way featuring two fake ghosts that are only bedsheets and one 'real' one with a person underneath, so they can reach out and grab at people just when they're feeling safe and unimpressed. Some dim lighting and one or two volunteers to snatch at our visitors when they walk through the tunnel we'll construct leading into the town hall, and that's my contribution made to the party, outside of bringing a dish and helping with clean-up. Hopefully it won't have to be any more complicated than that.

October 12th 1934

Well: it was worse than I expected.

Ethel and her puppet master, Pastor Collins, came to the meeting with three ideas and all the smug intimidation tactics that Christ never taught, and one of their ideas hit *far* too close to home.

The least offensive, and the one I can stand allowing, is one against stealing that involves a hand getting cut off as punishment in the afterlife. Nevermind that there are countries who maim people like that for stealing even food when they're starving, nevermind that it is a tactic of slavers all over the world (and that it thus equates a supposedly loving Christian God with such villains), and nevermind that it might encourage the children to pick up knives and go chopping at each other—it was still somehow the least of three evils.

The other two ideas were themes on the dangers of love, between boys and girls, and between boys and men. On one hand, Ethel presented a nightmare manger, with a bloodied unmarried woman (I would call her The Un-Mary-ied, but not out loud, I can't give these people more ideas) dying in a still-born childbirth. Perhaps in an effort to be fair (for lack of a better term), that scenario was presented as a room for girls, so they know the consequences of letting men anywhere near them, while the other room would be for boys, with a similar message and warning. In the boys' room, on a sweetheart's bench, instead of two courting young people, it would be one of the teenaged sons of the church being given flowers sweetly by a man in full demon regalia. When he accepts them without recoiling, fake flames pop up around him, the lights go red, and the demon strangles the boy with his whip-like tail.

I didn't know how else to argue except in their own terms, by being more anti-sex-than-thou, essentially. I told them that, "as a former teacher myself," every child has been tempted to steal, but not every child has an incipient lust just waiting to emerge for exploitation. Pastor Collins was pretty aggressive saying things like, "But isn't it important to warn young people of the dangers to come?"

and, "But don't you agree that these are *real* dangers?" He was like a salesman trying to get a 'yes' out of me because one 'yes' would start a snowball of bullying 'logic.' I neglected to mention that again, as a former teacher, I'd met my fair share of bullies as well, and knew how to deal with them.

The more I said, "Mr. Collins, that is not the question at hand," and, "Mr. Collins, my perception of dangers is not relevant here," the more I wanted a *Tom* Collins to steady my nerves. If only they'd brought a temperance idea to the table, that was a message even I might have used. I definitely tweaked Mr. Collins by calling him Mister instead of Pastor, as he badgered me until the end of the night when everyone said goodbye.

"Please, Mrs. Watson, it's *Pastor* Collins," he said, shaking my hand and thus holding me hostage.

"But you're not my pastor, *sir*," I said, before hustling out the door.

Behind me I heard him ask somewhat rhetorically, "And who is your pastor?" He sounded like he knew very well that I had no such man in my life. That is a fellow who not only doesn't mind making women uncomfortable, he enjoys it. Men like him make me practically miss the charm and grace of the acerbic Sherlock Holmes; he doesn't put people off maliciously, just naturally, and that will make a great deal of difference for Mr. Holmes if we all eventually come to Judgment Day.

Anyway: it's the anti-stealing horror show that will be the night's main stage attraction, and I'm going to borrow some of the fake blood in a syringe so I can make my vampiric neck wound squirt once or twice. We do not yet know if Holmes will arrive in time for the party, he does not have a telephone out in his seaside house, and has not sent a follow-up letter. He said he would arrive in October and I don't doubt his surety, even if he shows up at the eleventh hour on Halloween night, like the ghost from Watson's past that he is. Regardless, I heard from more than one woman that her husband would be dressing up as Sherlock Holmes for the party anyway, or at least dressing up in the fashion that he was drawn for Watson's stories. I suppose they intend it as a bit of fun on Watson, unless they instinctively know how terrifying it is to meet a man who might know all of your secrets. I certainly feel the occasional chill about it.

Wish me luck that I am not run out of town as a heretic after this party.

October 27th 1934

It's late, and I'm tired, and I'll have more to say once this night is finally over, but I will just note: I'm suspected not of heresy or witchcraft, but possible lesbianism and assault. More on the details later, I'm exhausted.

October 28th 1934

What a horror show!

The party started out well enough, normal, and nearly fun. Someone with a connection to the railroad got their hands on some dry ice and filled the room with spooky fog—wouldn't you know the one night England can't make her own fog is the one night it would be most appreciated, the night of our Halloween party?

My ghost idea did fine, my friends Carol and Minnie are the ones who agreed to come as my sisters in Satan with vampire costumes of their own. The children were contained safely indoors, and they were all freakishly delighted by every spray of fake blood, the dear little monsters. I talked with at least two men in deerstalker hats, neither of whom had even half the knowledge of Watson's stories, let alone any real semblance to the original Holmes. If the Great Man himself ever shows up as he promised our dear Watson he would, I shall regale him with sketches of these pretenders. Perhaps he will return the favor by clearing me of these spurious charges I face.

It was almost a nice evening. Watson and I found one another through the fog and the dark near the end. Everyone was kissing and hugging goodbye when a scream rang out, which was met by applause, all of us assuming it was someone giving us all a ghoulish send-off. Instead, out of the theatrical curtains of her anti-thievery morality play, came Ethel. She was clutching a young girl to her bosom, and crying bloody murder.

"She's been *blinded*! Blinded and interfered with! We need the police!"

That finally truly terrified the adults, as this girl was hardly ten or eleven years old, and she'd been blinded? She had blood all down a very sweet little angel costume, red staining white, and everyone rushed to her, the poor child's mother quickest of all.

"Look at me, Sarah, look at mommy!"

And indeed the girl did look at her mother, because she'd only been *temporarily* blinded. Someone had squirted her in the eyes with fake blood, and I looked to anger with Ethel then, because her histrionics had this girl's mother shaking with fear. Ethel saw my glare, and was incensed in turn that I would dare (I assume), which is how I got pinned with this so-called crime before the night was through.

"Someone put blood all over me and they took my purse, and my candy, and my earrings." Sarah's voice was so small, it broke my heart, and made her mother whimper and hold her tight.

"They blinded her so they could put their hands all over her," Ethel said. "I think we should lock down the building, I think we should search everyone for the girl's things, I really do think we need the police, she's been robbed!"

"The earrings were just a little birthday present from her grandmother, they weren't expensive," said our girl's mother. "They're certainly not worth putting her through any more trauma tonight, we're going home."

People tried to implore her to stay and solve the mystery, but no one had more strength than her will to take her child home to safety. Once she was gone, Ethel rounded on me saying something along the lines of, "Maybe if you hadn't fought so hard against our other ideas for tonight, this wouldn't have happened. Maybe you should be ashamed of yourself."

"Excuse me?" I asked her. "You say someone stole a little girl's earrings, and that's somehow my fault? I have my own earrings, I don't need to rob children for more."

"Taking her things was secondary," Ethel insisted. "When I found her she was so confused, she said there had been hands in the dark all over her body, snatching at her."

For some reason Ethel was telling me all of this. I nodded in acknowledgement and said, "You should tell her mother everything you know."

"What do you know, Mrs. Watson? She said it wasn't one of the other kids who did it, so it was either a man or it was a *woman*. Did I not see you squirting fake blood earlier? Is that not *evidence* of something?"

Sherlock Holmes she was not. I smirked at her, and that really enraged the woman. I knew what she was suspicious of by then: I had been so uncomfortable with her anti-sex plays that she now suspected me of reckless wantonness. How funny that I might be suspected of being a molester of girls when it was in sympathy with my husband, who is a lover of men (or at least one man) that prompted me to speak against their messages in the first place. It was so funny to me in that moment I nearly laughed. With Watson's secret in such plain sight, it was me, the most innocent bystander, who was suspected.

I don't like this but I don't think much will come of it in the end... unless it's some sort of elaborate frame-up. I did not touch the child, I don't have her earrings, and I'm not the only one who can't stand Ethel. Hopefully this will all blow over, and by this time next year I won't even remember the details about it except what I've recorded in this year's diary (you know who you are). It might all be sorted out by Halloween proper, and if not, then maybe Sherlock Holmes will earn his keep and solve it for us.

November 1st 1934

Halloween was a mess. Despite our best efforts to provide everyone with a safe and wholesome night so they wouldn't go out hell-raising on their own, it didn't work: not only was 'Hell-Home' blemished by little Sarah getting robbed, but there was vandalism on Halloween proper, the absolute least of which was Ethel's post box being stolen off her house. I mean... there was news over the wire from America, that in New Britain, Connecticut on Halloween night, a fourteen-year-old boy was beaten so badly by about twenty hoodlums he had a fractured skull. In another town a six-year-old girl died from a fire set by a candle placed in a jack-o-lantern. Yet still somehow *Ethel* is aggrieved today. She's been personally wronged and targeted, and she demands justice. Good luck to anyone trying to have their own tragedy around that woman, she's too jealous of the spotlight.

I remember her getting the post box in the first place, because she wasn't comfortable with the mail slot the rest of us have—it was an access portal to her home where her precious children live, and it wasn't safe enough for her. They replaced their door and hung a small storage box for letters just to the side of the door. They put a lock on the box's lid, but with nothing more than a nail holding it onto the house, now it's been nabbed. At least she can't suspect me of that, I had an alibi for the night of Halloween. *I* was drinking too much at Carol's house on the other side of town. I was at her party alone because Watson was otherwise occupied himself with his own friend.

Because: Sherlock Holmes did indeed loom up out of the shadows of October just when Watson and I were about to leave for Carol's. I left them with the house to themselves, and I made sure I got too toasted on gin punch to get myself back home at all—I wasn't interested in interrupting the boys, so I stayed away all night and all morning, and breakfasted with the girls. Minnie came back this morning to lightly mock my condition and recommend her homemade hangover cure: glass of orange juice with a spoonful of honey after. I did as I was told and found my stomach churned less and the sugar calmed me. I'll remember it in the future.

Minnie also informed us that Ethel would be holding another meeting this evening to "stem the tide" of violence and vandalism.

"Imagine having that kind of free time," Carol said, shaking her head. Carol of course has three grown boys and two grandchildren and works as her husband's business secretary, and Minnie shook her head and clucked her tongue, because she holds a job as a seamstress and takes care of her elderly parents when she returns home every day.

"Must be nice, so much energy," Minnie said, while I only nodded my assent gently. I am a housewife to a retired man myself, so I have plenty of free time, but I don't spend it meddling in other people's houses; I read, I take exercise, I enjoy my friends, and sometimes I still privately tutor children who are struggling in their subjects for my charity to the community.

"Shall we go to this meeting?" I asked wearily.

Carol curled her gray-shot blonde hair over her ear and sighed at her coffee. "I'll go if you go," she said.

"*Can* you go?" Minnie asked, raising a heavy, dark eyebrow at me. She has one of the most severely sarcastic faces I've ever seen.

"I shall rally," I promised. "I'll try to bait Sherlock Holmes into attending, I bet he could solve all our domestic squabbles in one breath."

And indeed, I was right about that. On arriving back home I was greeted first by Watson, and then from around the corner came the diving hawk that is Sherlock Holmes. He mimed as if he were to kiss my cheek (while making absolutely no contact whatsoever), then remarked on my hangover and told me—unprompted, with no knowledge but what his bloodhound nose gave him—why oranges and honey worked.

"Pleased to see you don't try to treat the effects of over-intoxication with old wives tales. Oranges prompt your body to help neutralize the acid in your stomach, and the sugar in honey helps your body process the alcohol."

I was silent for a beat, bamboozled by his actual self as I always am for a moment, as he's like trying to be friends with a royal. He's only a human man of course, but the legend of him is also ever-present, and it takes a pause to refocus the lenses in one's mind so that both images come together.

"It was orange *juice*, actually," was all I managed to say.

"Quite," he agreed, before disappearing again, leaving Watson to ask me about my previous night, and discuss with me the news of the morning, as he walked me upstairs where I would bathe and change and put on my face for the rest of the day.

Now, about that Ethel meeting: it was a whirlwind.

Because I went, Watson followed after, and as Watson went, Holmes followed too, there was no more cajoling needed to get him in the meeting room. In we marched, to a room more often used to vote on party themes, on charities to grant proceeds to, and whether or not we needed road maintenance more or less than a more powerful fire hose. Today, however, it was the court of Ethel, with Mr. Collins there too, and Mr. Ethel Anderson pinning drawings onto a blackboard stand: Exhibit A, Sarah's missing earrings; Exhibit B, a local statue of Oliver Cromwell dressed in women's undergarments; Exhibit C, the Anderson's missing post box. Watson and I took some chairs along with a couple dozen others, including Sarah and her parents, Carol and Minnie up in front sitting together, and a person I assume was taking notes for the paper—I would bet a good deal of money that Ethel requested a reporter, that she was trying to make the news.

Ethel stood behind a portable podium at the front of the room, waiting for us all to settle. She watched me with a vague distaste on her face before she noted Watson beside me, and Holmes beside him. It took her a moment to realize who was this tall, aloof old codger who appeared unwilling to take a seat, looking over Watson like a gargoyle on top of a house. The sight of Holmes thrilled Ethel, caused her to become flustered, to blush. I smiled quite deeply, knowing that Holmes's attention would not be the kind she wanted, not at all.

Holmes squinted around, made a few assessments, and then leaned down between Watson and I to whisper, "Shall I end this meeting before it's even begun?"

Watson and I nodded, excited partly that we had brought the best advantage to this parlor game of a meeting. Holmes then cleared his throat, bringing the meeting to order before Ethel could raise her gavel.

"Hello, my name is Sherlock Holmes, and I think I can be of assistance to you. My old colleague Dr. Watson has provided me the details surrounding the incident of the Halloween party with... was it Celia?"

"Sarah," announced the girl's mother, jumping out of her seat, and bringing the girl by the hand to meet Holmes where he had strode during his introduction: in front of the blackboard where the evidence was pinned up.

"This is the girl?" Holmes asked.

Sarah, wide-eyed and silent, nodded yes.

"And these were your earrings?" he asked, pointing to the artist's rendering. Two little gems with two little posts, and backings that screwed onto them.

Sarah nodded again.

"And you told everyone that you were blinded by fake blood, searched, and then the earrings were gone once you were free?"

"Yes," said Ethel, inserting herself into the scene. "I was there moments after it happened. She was in such a state, to be set upon so suddenly in the dark and then left just as quickly, robbed and staggering. I was only glad I was there to help."

"It happened very fast, did it?" Holmes asked the girl.

Sarah gulped. "Yes."

"And these are exactly your earrings right here in this picture?"

Again Sarah said, "Yes."

Holmes moved around the girl, inspecting her earlobes on both sides, and then returned to standing in front of her, shaking his head in disappointment.

"She is lying," Holmes declared, and the color fell out of Sarah's face.

"How dare you, sir!" Ethel said, but Sarah's mother dropped down to eye-level and turned Sarah to face her, and gave her another stern look.

Without so much as a word from her mother, Sarah wilted under her glare and said, "I lost them, I'm sorry! I didn't want you to be mad at me!"

"Well, that has happened anyway, hasn't it, Sarah? And not just me, look at all these people who were so worried about you, why don't you apologize to them?"

Sarah, looking like she was being led in front of a firing squad, turned to the rest of the room and squeaked out, "I'm sorry, everybody."

We all grumbled collectively that it was okay, lesson learned, and then Sarah was escorted out by her poor, wearied mother. Then Ethel's show was down an act, and Mr. Ethel pulled down the page with the earrings drawn on it and started folding it into a paper airplane.

After a moment of silence, Mr. Pastor Collins piped up with, "How did you know?"

Had I been answering that question to a man of the cloth I might say something tart like, "The Lord spoke to me." Holmes only answered him honestly.

"The earrings would have had to be delicately unscrewed from the girl's ears in the chaotic dark, and since her ear lobes hadn't been damaged in any way, and she said repeatedly that the theft happened quickly, logic dictates that there was no attack, and she would have known that to be true."

A light smattering of applause, and then Ethel tried to rally her issue when the most impressive incident was now off the board and sailing towards a wastepaper basket in the corner of the room (it fell short).

"Perhaps you can help us with the culprits of this, my missing post box?" she asked.

Holmes shrugged. "That is a personal matter, and I'm so sorry to say, I am retired."

With that he walked out of the room, and Watson and I had no choice but to follow him.

Ah, but we did grin merrily at one another as soon as we were back outside, somehow both of us proud of Holmes when we had nothing to do with his deductions. Mostly we had the pride of ambassadors I think, that in our boring little part of the world, we were the Bringers of Holmes. I was also particularly pleased to know that Ethel was back there in that meeting room with a sour face and nothing to say anymore. Go suck a lemon, Ethel.

*

On return home, the three of us had lunch. Holmes, Watson, and myself around one table, chewing silently, but the silence was almost comfortable. Holmes at this point is like no other guest in the world to us, neither family exactly nor friend exactly, but strangely comfortable like someone well-known in childhood who's been gone from your life for years, and yet still fits in it when they come back, weathered by the world.

We retired to the sitting room after lunch, as that's just when the sun begins to strike it and warm it up, and everyone took to reading or contemplating their own material. I was reading *Dracula's Guest and Other Weird Stories*, not because I find much value in it, but because I wanted to point the cover at Holmes to remind him that he owed me a story about Bram Stoker's secrets.

"Dracula's Guest" is no sequel, only a chapter removed from the original book where Jonathan Harker, *en route* to the Count's castle, decides to go wandering through an unholy village (as one does on a trip to a new country?), and during a thunderous storm, stumbles inside a tomb with a remarkably undead looking female body. When lightning strikes and the structure goes up in flames, he hears her scream. Then after some devil-wolf befriends him, he continues on his journey to Count Dracula's castle. It was not valuable to the story I'd already read, but it was published after Stoker's death by his wife, and there's no harm in that. Someday, barring untimely accident to myself, I shall have the same duty to my husband's legacy.

I was about to do something more obvious than pointing the *Dracula* cover at Holmes in a way that was unnatural for any human to read any book, honestly, but he finally ended my fretting. Holmes took a stack of fastened papers from his side table, folded them open to a previously marked page, and turned to me with the mild curiosity and laser precision of an owl.

"I see you have an interesting volume there, Mrs. Watson. I wonder if you remember something I mentioned the last time we met concerning Bram Stoker and Walt Whitman?"

Of course I remembered. Watson had more or less forgotten all about it, but perked up from some travel narrative about Africa the moment Holmes started to speak. He would recall what Holmes and I both already knew soon enough.

"I think I do remember that, Mr. Holmes; are you at all in a story-telling mood?" I asked. I would have made a terrible actress, I could hardly stand my own partial ruse, but Holmes didn't insist on it any further, he simply leaned over to hand me the pages he held on his lap and then sat back.

"We might start where we left off," Holmes said, as my eyes passed over some handwritten notes. "I did say that Bram Stoker had written some rather revealing letters to Walt Whitman? Well, there they are." I looked up startled before Holmes clarified. "Not the originals, of course not, but a fair copy of them, and the notes that Horace Traubel took around them while collecting as much information as he could during Whitman's final years. I wrote to Traubel's estate and had some of the notes copied out for my personal use, I thought I would arrive this time bearing gifts for the Watsons."

To say I was flattered is an understatement. I mean, of course he would not have gone to such effort for me alone, but it wasn't the pages I cared about so much as how he addressed us. There we were: the Watsons. Holmes saw Watson as joined with me, and me with him, so much as to say so explicitly. I think he and I knew that we would intentionally bring about another story time, as we had done so by accident when Holmes last visited. It made Watson so happy then, and we were both prepared to use artifice to see that happiness again. I felt like a bit of a conspirator with Holmes, and I must say, I do understand why Watson values that confidence so—being in the know with Sherlock Holmes is to be in the most exclusive club in all of England.

"Shall I read aloud?" I looked to Holmes first, then my husband. "Watson, would you be interested?"

"Yes, indeed," Watson said, and turned his chair to close our little circle. In that moment I dreaded the dinner bell, knowing that it would eventually interrupt our fun.

"Horace put out a few volumes of information like this before he died," Holmes explained as Watson settled down and I focused through my reading glasses. "His devotees are working to produce the rest, but no one has the same zeal as Horace did, so while these might be published someday, we all might not live to see it. Hopefully you'll each enjoy this previewing of the materials."

This will come as no surprise: we most certainly did enjoy them. Holmes is under strict orders not to spread around the pages, so I shall copy out the relevant bits here of what I read to them. It starts with notes from Mr. Horace Traubel about the moment when Whitman gave him these letters, and some explanation about their order and significance:

> I said to W.: "You don't feel like talking tonight: I'll skip off."
> He said: "I'm not spry, to be sure, but then you are always a tonic to me: don't hurry off just yet." Then he put on his glasses. "I've got something for you to do anyhow: after you do that you may go if you feel so disposed."

> *After turning over a lot of papers on the table he handed*
> *me some stuff pinned together.*
> *"Look at it: look it over: I rooted it out of a hole today while*
> *I was after something else."*
> *"It looks tasty," I said. He was very jolly over it.*

I first stopped reading right there, because I had to look at Watson and wonder (non-verbally) just what we were in for.

"Tasty," Watson said, considering it as if it was a whole new word he'd never thought of before.

"Tasty," I said back to him, before steeling myself to read on, I hoped without blushing.

Holmes said nothing, only sat back and observed us—bony ankle over bony knee, his whiter-each-year eyebrows arched high and reserved over his keen (if a tad cloudy) eyes.

I rejoined the document with Walt Whitman's answer:

> *"From your point of view it is tasty." I examined it. W. said:*
> *"I can easily tell you what it is: I want you to read it all to*
> *me: there are three letters: you have heard of Bram Stoker—*
> *Irving's man: he took a shine to me over there in Ireland*
> *when he was in college: wrote me from there—but was afraid*
> *to mail the letter: the second letter tells about it: he has been*
> *here: I value his good will highly: he seems to have remained*
> *of the same mind, mainly in substance, as at first."*
> *I continued turning it over. "Am I to read it?" I asked.*
> *"If you will," he said. There were two Stoker letters and the*
> *draft of a letter from W. acknowledging them.*
> *"It's a rather long story," I said: "there are several chapters*
> *to it."*

That is true, and I'll be condensing those chapters down here, to save my hand from cramp.

Then I read. Stoker's last letter first, then his first letter, then Walt's reply.

Dublin, Feb. 14, 1876.
My dear Mr. Whitman.
I hope you will not consider this letter from an utter stranger a liberty. Indeed, I hardly feel a stranger to you, nor is this the first letter that I have written to you. My friend Edward Dowden has told me often that you like new acquaintances or I should rather say friends. And as an old friend I send you an enclosure which may interest you. Four years ago I wrote the enclosed draft of a letter which I intended to copy out and send to you—it has lain in my desk since then—when I heard that you were addressed as Mr. Whitman. It speaks for itself and needs no comment. It is as truly what I wanted to say as that light is light. The four years which have elapsed have made me love your work fourfold, and I can truly say that I have ever spoken as your friend. You know what hostile criticism your work sometimes evokes here, and I wage a perpetual war with many friends on your behalf. But I am glad to say that I have been the means of making your work known to many who were scoffers at first. The years which have passed have not been uneventful to me, and I have felt and thought and suffered much in them, and I can truly say that from you I have had much pleasure and much consolation—and I do believe that your open earnest speech has not been thrown away on me or that my life and thought fail to be marked with its impress. I write this openly because I feel that with you one must be open. We have just had tonight a hot debate on your genius at the Fortnightly Club in which I had the privilege of putting forward my views—I think with success. Do not think me cheeky for writing this. I only hope we may sometime meet and I shall be able perhaps to say what I cannot write.

Dowden promised to get me a copy of your new edition and I hope that for any other work which you may have you will let me always be an early subscriber. I am sorry that you're not strong. Many of us are hoping to see you in Ireland. We had arranged to have a meeting for you. I do not know if you like getting letters. If you do I shall only be too happy to send you news of how thought goes among the men I know. With truest wishes for your health and happiness believe me
> *Your friend*
> *Bram Stoker.*

After going this far I waited for W. to say something. He was not disposed to talk.

"He was just about a boy back in those days: now it was fifteen years ago: he has been here: I think the man Stoker repeats, fulfils, the boy: I never quite think of myself as being the subject of such utterances. There's one sentence in his letter which hit me hard."

I said: "I'll bet I know which one it is."

He nodded. "I'm rather persuaded that you do: which?"

I quoted: "I write this openly—.»

W. interrupted me. "That's it: that's me, as I hope I am: it's Leaves of Grass *if* Leaves of Grass *is anything: 'I feel that with you one must be open': that explains* Children of Adam, *everything."*

I thought he might say more. He didn't. I gave him time. Then I read Stoker's first letter.

Dublin, Ireland, Feb. 18, 1872.
If you are the man I take you to be you will like to get this letter. [W. exclaimed: "I don't know that I'm the man he takes me to be, but I did like to get his letter—and I like to get it today again as you read it to me!"] If you are not

I don't care whether you like it or not and only ask you to put it into the fire without reading any farther. ["It has been here quite half a lifetime without getting into the fire!"] But I believe you will like it. ["I did, I do, like it!"] I don't think there is a man living, even you who are above the prejudices of the class of small-minded men, who wouldn't like to get a letter from a younger man, a stranger, across the world—a man living in an atmosphere prejudiced to the truths you sing and your manner of singing them. The idea that arises in my mind is whether there is a man living who would have the pluck to burn a letter in which he felt the smallest atom of interest without reading it. I believe you would and that you believe you would yourself. ["I don't know about that: I'm only about as weak and as strong as other people!"] You can burn this now and test yourself, and all I will ask for my trouble of writing this letter, which for all I can tell you may light your pipe with or apply to some more ignoble purpose—is that you will in some manner let me know that my words have tested your impatience. Put it in the fire if you like—but if you do you will miss the pleasure of this next sentence, which ought to be that you have conquered an unworthy impulse.

Now that is coming on a bit strong, if I do say so myself, but it is a charmingly boyish energy. I too have been pursued fervently once or twice by young men, and I never threw their letters into the fire either. Anyhow, more from Stoker:

A man who is uncertain of his own strength might try to encourage himself by a piece of bravo, but a man who can write, as you have written, the most candid words that ever fell from the lips of mortal man—a man to whose candor Rousseau's Confessions *is reticence—can have no fear for his own strength. If you have gone this far you may read the letter and I feel in writing now that I am talking to you. If I were before your face I would like to shake hands with you, for I feel that I would like you. I would like to call you Comrade and to talk to you as men who are not poets do not often talk.*

I stopped reading for a moment there, because my goodness, how romantic! I said as much to my Watson, and then read Whitman's comment on it too, saying, *"He was a sassy youngster: as to burning the epistle up or not—it never occurred to me to do anything at all: what the hell did I care whether he was pertinent or impertinent? he was fresh, breezy, Irish: that was the price paid for admission—and enough: he was welcome!"*

Stoker's letter continued, with maybe the sweetest line that remains repeating in my head still:

I think that at first a man would be ashamed, for a man cannot in a moment break the habit of comparative reticence that has become a second nature to him; but I know I would not long be ashamed to be natural before you.

Knowing how ashamed he must have felt at times, surrounded by hostile opinions of Whitman's work for the very nature of its feelings. To say to someone, sight unseen, *"I would not long be ashamed to be natural before you..."* What love there is in that.

You are a true man, and I would like to be one myself, and so I would be towards you as a brother and as a pupil to his master. ["There's 'master' again!"] In this age no man becomes worthy of the name without an effort. You have shaken off the shackles and your wings are free. ["My wings may be free but the same can't be said of my backside!"] I have the shackles on my shoulders still—but I have no wings. If you are going to read this letter any further I should tell you that I am not prepared to "give up all else" so far as words go. The only thing I am prepared to give up is prejudice, and before I knew you I had begun to throw overboard my cargo, but it is not all gone yet. I do not know how you will take this letter. I have not addressed you in any form as I hear that you dislike to a certain degree the conventional forms in letters. ["Not to a certain degree but altogether! and not only in letters: everywhere!"] I am writing to you because you are different from other men. If you were the same as the mass I would not write at all. As it is I must either call you Walt Whitman or not call you at all—and I have chosen the latter course.

The last I read today was Whitman's final thought on this introduction: "*The boy fires off a hell of a big prologue—eh? Horace?*" Truer words were never spoken, nor transcribed by me. I must continue tomorrow, because between the morning flurry, this mid-day reading, and dinner, the daylight has escaped me, and I can hardly read these notes at all by candlelight. Holmes has promised us more fascinations before he goes (whenever that will be, no one knows or no one's told me). I'll update you as soon as I can after that.

November 3rd 1934

This week, my word. Yesterday, Friday, Miss Tress went missing. I'm not one to cage a bird, you understand; if the creature doesn't want to be with us, she's wild and smart enough to take her freedom, but she did seem to prefer a warm home and free food, and it just wasn't like her to be entirely missing from dinner time. Sometimes she arrived late, more often she'd pester me for food early, but she's never skipped a meal entirely.

Friday morning her food was still sitting in her bowl by the door. It's too cold for the bugs to have found it, but the nice morsels we put out for her were dried up, desiccated, and then she didn't appear all day. I told Watson I'd be going out at dusk with some food to call for her, and he better not try to stop me. He didn't try to stop me, but he did enlist Holmes in a search, called it his most impossible case yet: how to find a missing cat who may not want to be found. Holmes got up and went straight to his boots, probably because it was a good time for an evening constitutional anyway, but as we walked out the door, he took up storytelling again.

"You heard Walt Whitman refer to Mr. Stoker as Irving's man, do either of you know whom he was referring to?"

I was scanning scrubby flora along the road looking for the movement or soft lump of a cat, so Watson took up answering for this pop quiz.

"The great stage actor Henry Irving, Bram Stoker was his attendant or personal assistant or stage manager or something, wasn't he?"

"All that and more," Holmes said, "for years and years. I don't think it was anywhere near as happy a partnership as ours though, Watson, nowhere near as reciprocal."

I purposely didn't look round at that claim, because Holmes and Watson were never really equals as partners under any definition, but they were happy at times. So much more's the pity for Mr. Stoker.

"He was overwhelmed by the man, enchanted by him?" Watson guessed. Watson very easily guessed.

"Yes," Holmes confirmed. "So he wrote years later in his book, *Personal Reminiscences of Henry Irving*. He said the first evening he truly met and interacted with Irving was so memorable because it began, so he called it, 'the close friendship between us which only terminated with his life if indeed friendship, like any other form of love, can ever terminate.'"

"So sentimental, was he?" Watson asked with a smile of approval. "Thinking that love can never die?"

I couldn't help by chime in then with, "I wonder what his wife's opinion was on the subject of undying love." Probably not so starry-eyed, is my guess, but only because I've gleaned from Holmes that not only was this the *second* man of a certain secret persuasion that asked for Florence Balcombe's hand in marriage (Oscar Wilde was the first), but either one of them could have infected her with syphilis in the end, unless, as rumors suggest, the Irish beauty kept her husband out of her bedchambers after the conception of their child, and he then caught his syphilis elsewhere as a result of that rebuff.

"Stoker had written about one of Irving's performances before," Holmes continued, "and the actor, as actors are wont to do, remembered every good word printed about him just as well as the bad. Stoker had written good things, and for that was invited to a private party with Irving's coterie, where according to Stoker, Mr. Irving's heart was 'beginning something toward me, as mine had been toward him' because 'he had learned that I could appreciate high effort.' After dinner Irving said he would like to recite Thomas Hood's poem 'The Dream of Eugene Aram' for Bram, and so he did."

The evening night fell down a notch then, and I saddened thinking I'd never spot Miss Tress in the dark, I could only call out to her, but was then again reluctant to interrupt Holmes's story with calls and coos of, 'Where's my Miss *Tress*, where *is* my Miss *Tress*?' I mostly hoped she would be home before us and demanding double dinner by the time we got back to the house. I managed to keep up with the general conversation though.

I asked Holmes, "Was Bram Stoker in love before Henry Irving finished the first stanza?"

Watson laughed, and Holmes nodded firmly, either in approval of Watson's amusement or because indeed that is what happened during that performance. I got the details a bit later from Stoker's book (I swear our library is bigger on the inside than it is on the outside). Stoker wrote of that magical night, saying:

> *That experience I shall never—can never—forget. The recitation was different, both in kind and degree, from*

anything I had ever heard; and in those days there were some noble experiences of moving speech. It had been my good fortune to be in Court when Whiteside made his noble appeal to the jury in the Yelverton Case [...] I had heard Lord Brougham speak amid a tempest of cheers in the great Round Room of the Dublin Mansion House. I had heard John Bright make his great oration on Ireland in the Dublin Mechanics' Institute, and had thrilled to the roar within and the echoing roar from the crowded street without which followed his splendid utterance [...]

But here in a hotel drawing-room, amid a dozen friends, a man in evening dress stood up to recite a poem with which we had all been familiar from our schooldays, which most if not all of us had ourselves recited at some time. But such was Irving's commanding force, so great was the magnetism of his genius, so profound was the sense of his dominance that I sat spellbound. Outwardly I was as of stone; nought quick in me but receptivity and imagination. That I knew the story and was even familiar with its unalterable words was nothing. The whole thing was new, recreated by a force of passion which was like a new power. [...]

There are great moments even to the great. That night Irving was inspired. Many times since then I saw and heard him—for such an effort eyes as well as ears are required—recite that poem and hold audiences, big or little, spellbound till the moment came for the thunderous outlet of their pent-up feelings; but that particular vein I never met again. Art can do much; but in all things even in art there is a summit somewhere. That night for a brief time in which the rest of the world seemed to sit still, Irving's genius floated in blazing triumph above the summit of art. There is something in the soul which lifts it above all that has its base in material things. If once only in a lifetime the soul of a man can take wings and sweep for an instant into mortal gaze, then that "once" for Irving was on that, to me, ever memorable night.

As to its effect I had no adequate words. I can only say that after a few seconds of stony silence following his collapse I burst out into something like a violent fit of hysterics. Let me say, not in my own vindication, but to bring new tribute to Irving's splendid power, that I was no hysterical subject. I was no green youth; no weak individual, yielding to a superior emotional force. I was as men go a strong man, strong in many ways. If autobiography is allowable in a work of reminiscence let me say here what I was:

I was a very strong man. It is true that I had known weakness. In my babyhood I used, I understand to be, often at the point of death. [...] This early weakness, however, passed away in time and I grew into a strong boy and in time enlarged to the biggest member of my family. When I was in my twentieth year I was Athletic Champion of Dublin University. When I met Irving first I was in my thirtieth year. I had been for ten years in the Civil Service and was then engaged on a dry-as-dust book on The Duties of Clerks of Petty Sessions. I had edited a newspaper, and had exercised my spare time in many ways as a journalist; as a writer of short and serial stories; as a teacher. In my College days I had been Auditor of the Historical Society a post which corresponds to the Presidency of the Union in Oxford or Cambridge and had got medals, or certificates, for History, Composition and Oratory. I had been President of the Philosophical Society; had got Honours in pure Mathematics. I had won numerous silver cups for races of various kinds. I had played for years in the University football team, where I had received the honour of a "cap!" I was physically immensely strong. In fact I feel justified in saying I represented in my own person something of that aim of university education mens sana in corpore sano. *When, therefore, after his recitation I became hysterical, it was distinctly a surprise to my friends; for myself surprise had no part in my then state of mind. Irving seemed much moved by the occurrence.*

So: it wasn't Walt Whitman particularly that made Mr. Stoker so verbose and over-the-top affectionate, but maybe it did have something to do with powerful men, as later that night Holmes gathered us again for the rest of the introduction letter Stoker had written to Whitman. This evening it was Watson who did the reading aloud, as I was still distracted looking out the window for Miss Tress (she is still not returned), and worrying over whether the Halloween mayhem had gotten to the point of animal sacrifice or something (I'm still a little worried, but trying not to obsess over what I cannot control—I'll go out cat-seeking alone before dawn).

Anyway, the rest of the Stoker letter to Whitman resumed with even more of his braggadocio, as if Mr. Stoker was posting an ad of himself and his tasty manly qualities, trying to find another great man who would take him. Watson took up where I left off:

I don't know whether it is usual for you to get letters from utter strangers who have not even the claim of literary brotherhood to write you. If it is you must be frightfully tormented with letters and I am sorry to have written this. I have, however, the claim of liking you—for your words are your own soul and even if you do not read my letter it is no less a pleasure to me to write it. Shelley wrote to William Godwin and they became friends. I am not Shelley and you are not Godwin and so I will only hope that sometime I may meet you face to face and perhaps shake hands with you. If I ever do it will be one of the greatest pleasures of my life.

If you care to know who it is that writes this, my name is Abraham Stoker (Junior). My friends call me Bram. I live at 43 Harcourt St., Dublin. I am a clerk in the service of the Crown on a small salary. I am twenty-four years old. Have been champion at our athletic sports (Trinity College, Dublin) and have won about a dozen cups. I have also been President of the College Philosophical Society and an art and theatrical critic of a daily paper. I am six feet two inches high and twelve stone weight naked and used to be forty-one or forty-two inches round the chest.

"Whoa," I interrupted there, because honestly: whoa. Methinks Mr. Stoker dearly lacked the womanly art of subtlety. Watson met my gaze with his own wide-eyed look of surprise, smoothed his mustache nervously, and then continued. Holmes meanwhile was gazing into the fire as if he was not hearing us at all, though of course I know that he was more than aware of everything surrounding him. The letter carried on:

I am ugly but strong and determined and have a large bump over my eyebrows. I have a heavy jaw and a big mouth and thick lips—sensitive nostrils—a snubnose and straight hair. I am equal in temper and cool in disposition and have a large amount of self control and am naturally secretive to the world. I take a delight in letting people I don't like—people of mean or cruel or sneaking or cowardly disposition—see the worst side of me. I have a large number of acquaintances and some five or six friends—all of which latter body care much for me. Now I have told you all I know about myself.

Whitman interjected then, *"And a mighty graphic picture it is too: I seem to see you not as in a glass darkly but as in the broad day lightly:*

I do, I do!" Stoker's rambling continued on, but I won't include it all. Instead, the next moving bit was Stoker's description of Whitman's poetry, and how it affected him, when everyone else he knew mocked the very subject.

> *I took home the volume and read it far into the night. Since then I have to thank you for many happy hours, for I have read your poems with my door locked late at night, and I have read them on the seashore where I could look all round me and see no more sign of human life than the ships out at sea: and here I often found myself waking up from a reverie with the book lying open before me. I love all poetry, and high generous thoughts make the tears rush to my eyes, but sometimes a word or a phrase of yours takes me away from the world around me and places me in an ideal land surrounded by realities more than any poem I ever read. [...]*
>
> *Be assured of this, Walt Whitman—that a man of less than half your own age, reared a conservative in a conservative country, and who has always heard your name cried down by the great mass of people who mention it, here felt his heart leap towards you across the Atlantic and his soul swelling at the words or rather the thoughts. It is vain for me to try to quote any instances of what thoughts of yours I like best—for I like them all and you must feel that you are reading the true words of one who feels with you. You see, I have called you by your name. I have been more candid with you—have said more about myself to you than I have ever said to any one before. You will not be angry with me if you have read so far. You will not laugh at me for writing this to you. It was with no small effort that I began to write and I feel reluctant to stop, but I must not tire you any more. If you ever would care to have more you can imagine, for you have a great heart, how much pleasure it would be to*

me to write more to you. How sweet a thing it is for a strong
healthy man with a woman's eyes and a child's wishes to
feel that he can speak so to a man who can be if he wishes
father, and brother and wife to his soul. I don't think you
will laugh, Walt Whitman, nor despise me, but at all events
I thank you for all the love and sympathy you have given me
in common with my kind.
    —Bram Stoker.

"My God," Watson said, as he lowered the page.

"A man with a woman's eyes," I repeated to Watson, knowing precisely what that meant, what such eyes found pleasure in gazing upon.

"Father, and brother, and wife to his soul," Watson said, nodding and agreeing with me. That is a very difficult person to find, the one who can embody all that another soul desires. Watson has not found it; I have not found it. In Watson I have a friend and husband, in me he has a friend and wife, but my brothers are all gone, lost in the war, my father long dead and always distant, more focused on his boys. Whatever Holmes is to Watson, I doubt he would ever use the words "father" or "brother" to describe him. Holmes to Watson is what Henry Irving was to Stoker: a summit of mankind, a wonder. Watson to Holmes was at times a brother, a wife, but never a father (his blood-brother Mycroft was that), and so there we all were: three people in one room, bringing all that we had to the table, and building what we needed from the pieces that we found.

"Sympathy with his own kind," Holmes said, as his take-away from the letter. I could have hugged him for that, in the moment, for that is as dear a treasure as any, and I do believe we three have it.

Whitman's response to Stoker was much shorter (bless him), addressed Stoker as "my dear young man" and thanked him for the fresh, manly affection of his words. Whitman wrote, "My physique is entirely shattered—doubtless permanently, from paralysis and other ailments. But I am up and dressed, and get out every day a little. Live here quite lonesome, but hearty, and good spirits. Write to me again."

Whitman too hoped that they would one day meet, and indeed they did, more than once. Holmes said there was one last amusing note he'd like to give us on the topic of Bram Stoker and Walt Whitman, but insisted that he hold onto it until he departs from our house (the showman). We retired then, me to my diary and Holmes and Watson to whatever quiet things they do with one another, and I shall now go to bed early so I can wake in time to go cat-hunting.

November 4th 1934

The important news is: I've found Miss Tress, and she is fine. The ridiculous news is that I *knew*, I knew instinctively, that calling through the dark desperately seeking my "Miss Tress" would put me in some socially awkward misunderstanding, and I have the previously dated entry to prove it. I was going through the darkness with my torch in hand when I spotted her, crouching and guarded underneath a car, and when she moved off into the brush to avoid me I followed her. She was injured, you see, some other animal had caught hold of her leg, and the precious creature was afraid of any more interaction with large beasts of the world, including myself. I followed her without noticing where I was going, into whose property or proximity I crossed. Naturally, of course, I ended up cooing for my sweet and darling Miss Tress outside of Ethel's home, and of course it was right at the pale top of dawn when she was out unhooking washing from the line on her porch, and of course when she saw me out half-dressed and crawling around after my Miss Tress, she crossed her arms and let an ugly look settle onto her face.

"Out playing dirty games with our mistress, are we?" she asked.

I had just found Miss Tress somewhere I could contain her (a fallen rubbish bin with a lid nearby), and was royally unamused to be distracted at such a critical moment. In an instant I registered

Ethel, my grubby, dirty appearance in her yard, the fact that I was just about to steal what was surely her rubbish bin, and knew that I would be the talk of the town for a day or two, but didn't care. I had seen Miss Tress limping. My passing embarrassment was nothing compared to the importance of getting that cat home safely and evaluated by my sweet healer of a husband. I didn't care what Ethel saw, or thought she saw, or what she'd tell others; the truth was on my side, and for a moment I was unashamed.

I could have pointed out that I was after my cat, that no grown woman mistress would find this cold rush through brambles and mud a sexy game to play, but I wasn't going to stand there and argue with Ethel, or lend her stupidity any validity by trying to gain its approval. Instead, I took the sarcastic route.

"Well, you've finally caught me," I said, as I picked up the bin lid and approached the fallen trash can crouched down like a huntress. "Guess I'll expect the police at the door later today for my cat-calling lasciviousness."

There's a good chance Ethel didn't even know that word before she heard me say it. She stayed silent as I secured my trash cat, and then started off for home with Miss Tress caterwauling within.

"That is *my property* you have there," Ethel finally said, and it sounded like she was pulling a knotted scarf out of her mouth.

"Bill me!" I shouted back, and then spent the walk home wondering how much hell I'd have to catch for my smart mouth come daylight.

I was being talked about, of course. Carol and Minnie both reached out to make sure I was aware of the gossip, but I was unconcerned about that, blissfully interested only in changing Miss Tress's bandage. Watson returned the rubbish bin to Ethel's house, and I'm sure his charm did some soothing of the drama, but I didn't concern myself with human problems, only tended the cat and was happy to find her much more loving when she realized I was there to help her. I think at long last she agrees to be our pet and no one else's—I've proved my devotion.

It's been Cat City in the Watson household today, and I do not know where or what Holmes did, but I'm sure he's heard about me, as I've become notorious. I think Holmes is leaving soon if he hasn't already—as much as I want that last bit of Stoker gossip, I'm not letting Miss Tress feel unloved to get it, the man knows how to write a letter, after all, and besides which, I may know enough about Mr. Stoker for the rest of my days now, as I suddenly remembered that he was quite conservative in his later years.

Long after Whitman and Wilde were both dead, Stoker had changed his tune. I actually found the note of my previous outrage in my diary from 1909, as that was the year I had wanted to take a holiday to Ireland, and never quite managed to pull it off. In my own bitterness, I contented myself instead with trying to dislike the place, and Stoker's article called "The Censorship of Stage Plays" went a long way in helping me do just that. According to my notes, Stoker argued vociferously in favor of the censorship of stage plays, saying that people must "take militant actions... against such movements of reaction and decadence as are made by the defenders of indecency of thought and action... were such base efforts continuous, some effective means of repression and punishment would have to be brought to bear."

Oscar Wilde was punished, severely, in no small part due to the "indecency" of his plays, his work, his art. Stoker could be *very* long ashamed in front of a man like Walt Whitman for promoting something like that, but perhaps he grew bitter instead of better in old age. Irving had refused to stage Stoker's *Dracula* by then (thought it was trash, beneath him); Stoker's marriage was unhappy, and he had only himself to thank for pursuing a woman who had still been engaged to Wilde at the time; he lived perhaps in cowardly fear that what ultimately happened to Wilde might happen to him too, if he wasn't vehement enough, reticent enough, self-loathing enough to deflect suspicion.

Whatever Stoker's reasons, they were much uglier motives than what brought him to Walt Whitman as a young man, and it makes me tired to think of how quickly life can wear down our better urges into bitter unctuousness.

November 5th 1934

Happy Guy Fawkes Day! Ethel has been deemed annoying by more than just me, so her bleating about my behavior is only holding sway with her church group, and of that set only Pastor Mister Collins is enough of a personality to make any ingress with others. I would have been more concerned about that, except for Holmes's parting gift this morning. On securing his shoes and packing his pipe for his outgoing journey, Holmes first gave us the bit of information he'd teased about Bram Stoker, who after years of being friends with Whitman, got one last bequeath from him. Holmes brought our attention to another page of *Personal Reminiscences of Henry Irving* that he had marked out, a section which read:

> We did not reach Philadelphia till towards the end of January 1894. In the meantime Walt Whitman had died, March 26, 1892. On 4th February I spent the afternoon with [Thomas] Donaldson in his own home. Shortly after I came in he went away for a minute and came back with a large envelope which he handed to me: 'That is for you from Walt Whitman. I have been keeping it till I should see you.' The envelope contained, in a rough card folio, pasted down on thick paper, the original notes from which Whitman delivered his lecture on Abraham Lincoln at the Chestnut Street Opera House on April 15, 1886. With it was a letter to Donaldson, in which he said: 'Enclosed I send a full report of my Lincoln Lecture for our friend Bram Stoker.' This was my Message from the Dead.

Watson's first response was something along the lines of, "Isn't he morbid, saying a 'Message from the Dead'?" While my first response was, "Another lover of Lincoln, I see."

Holmes grinned, the same grin of every man who thinks he has taught me well, from my father, my brothers, my husband. After sweeping his hat and coat on, Holmes bent his head closer to mine for one extra secret.

"I have a gift for you," Holmes said. "I know who stole that loud woman's post box. It was taken by her pastor; they're having an affair."

And with a light smirk and a wink he was gone again, and I was laughing so hard that Watson was taking my temperature, worried about my health and sanity.

Watson asked me, "What has overcome you?"

I told him, between gasping breaths, that I was only surprised. "It's just a mild case of shock, darling," I wheezed and huffed. "That was the nicest thing Sherlock Holmes has ever said to me."

Felo De Se

Watson and I were beginning to dust off our Christmas decorations when there was a knock on our door, an unexpected guest. They did not knock with a fist, but with a cane or object of some sort, making it less likely that it was one of our neighbors. Usually that meant it could be no one other than Sherlock Holmes, but when I answered the door, I didn't recognize the man I found. White-bearded, bald-headed, and when I sought his eyes to ask to whom I had the pleasure of speaking, I found a man who looked devastated.

"I... sir, are you...?"

That was all I could say before Watson walked up behind me to see who it was, and the man spotted him, and the sorrow in his eyes deepened. I got out of the way as this man and my Watson went for a bear of a hug. I shut the door behind him and started thinking in hosting logistics. I snatched off his hat, stole his cane, and tugged at his jacket when the hug was complete so he would shrug it off. I scurried away to put a kettle on and clear the sitting room of our dusty holiday boxes, all before I was aware of who this fellow was.

Watson installed the man by our fire, cupped my elbows so that I would follow him into the kitchen, and there at least one mystery was revealed.

"That is Colonel Hayter," Watson said. "I don't believe you've ever met, but maybe you remember who..."

I peeked through the kitchen door to see if I could spot a sliver of him. "I know who he is, and no, we've never met."

Colonel Hayter is a former patient of Watson's from Afghanistan, though he might be known by my husband's readers as the man from "The Adventure of the Reigate Squire," a mystery in which Holmes was embroiled while he was supposed to be recovering from a particularly strenuous international case in 1887. The lesser-known secret of Holmes's ill health was that he was fueled with cocaine at the time, so it was both rest and rehabilitation that he needed during his stay at Colonel Hayter's estate.

Holmes rebelled at the thought of rest and rehab, but he found recreation with Colonel Hayter, flirting and fornicating with him right under Watson's nose when it was clear as day that Hayter had held a small flame for Watson for years (why else be so generous as to host him and his messy, famous friend), while meanwhile Watson was terribly in love with Holmes. It was a prism of betrayal, every which way you turned the situation it was Holmes being selfish, petulant, malicious, and mean, when all involved were only there to help him deal with his own personal failings. I think that was the problem, that Holmes was revealed to have the same dirty human frailties as anyone else, and there were two men who knew that about him enough to take pity, to lend compassion. They were punished for knowing too much, even as Holmes had to accept their help.

When I first heard of the true circumstances behind it all I was furious with Holmes, and still am, when I think about it too much. Nevermind that it happened almost fifty years ago, long before Watson ever met me, when I was barely a person to be met at all, only fourteen years old. When he told me about it, I was outraged on Watson's behalf, and mad at him for being the kind of man whose kindness could be so trod upon, and now here was Colonel Hayter himself, like a creature from a story long-forgotten but still deeply felt. Frankenstein's poor monster come to life, in emotional distress, and in need of help.

I took a few moments to marshal my thoughts. The past is the past, I reminded myself. Holmes wasn't here, but even if he was, he was not the man he used to be, and neither was Watson, otherwise I wouldn't be here at all. Who was here? Colonel Hayter, and whatever was happening to him wasn't about some misadventure from half a century ago, it was something much more recent and raw. He was holding back tears in my house, and I didn't even know his first name.

"What's his name, dear?" I asked.

"Reginald," Watson said.

Regimental Reginald, he was where my emotional energy should be directed, not in flailing at a past long-gone and almost forgotten.

"Did he tell you what happened to him?"

"Someone died, an old friend of his," Watson said. "It was suicide, he put his old Webley under his chin."

A Webley was the standard issue service revolver for our boys in the Great War. I hate to think of how many of them were eventually turned on their owners or other citizens here at home.

"Was he... were they... close?" I asked. Watson knew what I meant.

"That I don't know yet. I think we better keep him here for as long as he wants to stay though, don't you?"

"Of course," I said. God forbid we turn him away and there's another suicide to hear about, no no no, not if my cordiality could help it.

As I spied Colonel Hayter, he was surprised out of his mile-long stare into the fireplace when our cat jumped suddenly into his lap and began rubbing her whiskers against his.

"Oh," said the old colonel. He almost smiled as he let our soft creature invade his face space. I smiled to see him brought back to life a little.

"Miss Tress just jumped into his lap," I told Watson, turning from the door.

"Did she?" Watson moved to see for himself. "She doesn't like anyone. She barely tolerates us."

"She must reserve her affection for those who need it," I said. "Go make sure he's not allergic to her, I'll see about dinner."

Seeing about dinner, for me, meant phoning Maurice.

Though he worked for my father and then for my husband for many years as a cook, even Maurice, who at one time seemed timeless to me, was too old to work anymore. He was still willing to give me free advice though.

"Have you got company then?" he asked.

"In the very next room." I spoke loudly because it was necessary, hoping that I wouldn't have to say anything indiscreet to get the help that I needed.

"Male or female or couple?" Maurice asked.

"That first one sounds lovely," I said.

"Any meat in the house?"

"We have a bit of beef, some potatoes, an onion or two..."

"You're making a stew, then. Combine the meat and any veg you can find in a pot and get it cooking now. Use stock for flavor if you have it, if not, water, salt and pepper, flour to thicken it. Brown the meat first, make sure the liquid covers everything, bring to a broil, then let simmer for an hour or two."

"Got it," I said, as I took notes so I wouldn't forget it.

"And be sure to chop the vegetables into little bite-sized cubes before cooking them," Maurice said, with a creaky, knee-slapping laugh.

"Oh, ha, ha. I probably knew that."

"Probably, love. Call back if anything goes wrong and I'll try to help."

"Thanks, Maurice, you're too good to me," I told him.

"And too good for you my young missus, but I'm a generous old man."

Then it was kiss-kiss and we hung up. My marriage only turned me from 'young miss' to 'young missus' in his eyes. When my father died, Maurice was like having an uncle in the wings waiting to take on the mantle of Papa.

I set up the food, hoping that having something warm in our bellies would be enough even if it was kind of bland. Watson and I were in the habit of grazing our own dinners independently most nights, only going through the whole cooking and sit-down dining process when there were guests or special occasions. Tonight we had a surprise guest, so instead of bread softened under tinned beans by the fire, we were having stew instead. There aren't a lot of luxury items around these days, what with the world in such a precarious state all the time, but we still have enough food when we need it.

At last I rejoined the men, who were both sitting quietly, staring at the fire then, with half-drunk glasses of alcohol in their hands.

"What are we drinking?" I asked them. I was ready to join in.

"Here, let me." Watson got up and offered me his own seat as he went to top off their glasses and get me a drink as well. I was then face-to-face with Colonel Hayter, who looked as sad and weary as any man I'd ever seen.

"You've lost someone," I said to him. "I'm sorry."

"Thank you," Hayter said. "Though I wonder if it's fair to say I've lost him, when it was he who threw himself away."

Watson returned with the drinks and said, "That's not what happened. I believe you when you say he did it to himself, but a man doesn't live for sixty-some years and just drop his life into the bin like it was nothing, he wasn't nothing."

"Hmm," said Hayter, taking another sip of liquor. "I suppose that depends on who you ask, and what they knew about him, because..." Hayter stopped himself. He looked at me, then at Watson, who had just sat down in a third chair between us, completing a semi-circle around the fire's glow. "May I speak freely?"

Watson leaned to whisper for a while in Hayter's ear, and when he sat back he set his hand over mine and nodded to Hayter. Suddenly all eyes were on me again, and I smiled, nervous and knowing no other way to express it.

"He told you I keep a good secret, didn't he? Even Sherlock Holmes trusts me to keep tight-lipped."

"I think it's wonderful," Colonel Hayter said. "That Watson has you, that you both can be so honest with one another. "Silas's family won't know what really happened, he did a good job making it look like an accident, like he was cleaning his gun and it just went off by mistake, but he knew what he was doing. I was sure of it when I heard what happened, he talked about it enough times when we were in the war, saying that if he was left alive but mangled, the way to ensure a clean death was to shoot up." Hayter pointed to the space beneath his jaw right where his head met his neck. "My apologies for being graphic, ma'am, but the point is to get the bullet inside the skull without having to break through it first. Sometimes a bullet will glance off the skull, but if you can get it through the hole in the bottom, the bullet can bounce around inside like a damn pinball machine."

"That hole is called the foramen magnum," Watson told me. "In Latin it literally and simply means 'great hole.' It's the space the spinal cord passes through."

Watson was describing the anatomy of the human skull, and meanwhile I was picturing everyone's head like a pinball machine with its own inner themes and colors (galaxies, baseball diamonds, card tables, mythical mazes) and a bullet pinging around trying to find purchase, to find a place to rest itself so that you might… rest yourself.

"I also received this note from him the next day," Hayter said, and produced a tiny envelope with a heartbreakingly small amount of writing on the card inside.

Watson read it aloud. "I can't stand it anymore. I want to sleep a long time. Please don't follow me."

My heart was immediately in my throat, I couldn't speak lest I should start crying. My brother Everard was the one death I wondered about, amongst my own blood. In a war, it's hard to tell accident from suicide sometimes, and while officially his death was ruled as an accidental gun discharge, it was his own gun, held in his own hand. Perhaps it was an accident, perhaps it was a secret suicide, perhaps it was a known suicide covered up as an accident, there is truly no way to know for sure. What I do know is that his mother would have considered suicide a sin, as that is what her faith told her, so I'm only glad that (whatever the truth may be) the story the family received was one she could make peace with before she died of cancer. That being said, had I received a note like the one I just heard from Everard after he was gone, it would have hurt more.

It was Hayter who had the courage to speak first, after gesturing to have this last dispatch from a condemned soul returned to him.

"I hope I can trust both of you to keep this secret," he said. "The law considers suicide a crime against God and the Crown, and should his death be known as such, it could mean all his possessions would be forfeited to the government."

"That's… grim," Watson said. Even in death, one must pay one's taxes.

"Uglier still is when they punish an attempted suicide," Hayter said. "At least they can't reach beyond the grave, yet."

I almost laughed, not out of uncaring disrespect, mind you, but because the government would absolutely petition Heaven and Hell if it could, and because sometimes I laugh so that I do not weep, it's a mechanism of defense according to Freud. I believe I effectively hid my outburst as a cough.

"Of course, we'll want you to stay with us tonight," I said.

"That's right," Watson said. "For as many nights as you can stand our hospitality."

I nodded. "You should be among friends."

Watson is his friend, I by the transitive property of marriage am his friend, but there's one more we could call on if we wanted to, one more person who would understand, at least in part. Watson said his name first.

"Do you think Holmes would be of help here?" Watson asked me tonight, after dinner, and just after we'd left Colonel Hayter to his own private, murky thoughts.

"I honestly do not know, dear," I told him. We were disrobing for bed, performing our nightly rituals, I at my vanity alter and Watson over his scrying mirror. I laid out for him all the thoughts I had on the matter. "Would Holmes understand the sadness of this situation? Yes. Would he understand it enough to be sympathetic rather than pragmatic about wasted emotions? Debatable. Are he and Colonel Hayter at all on good terms? Unknowable without asking each of them. Might Holmes nevertheless spot some warning sign that would keep Hayter from following his friend into the dark? Probably. He'd certainly spot it quicker than you or I."

"That's what I'm most worried about," Watson said, coming to rest his hands on my shoulders. "That the Colonel won't heed that note, that this will be the one battle he surrenders."

"I don't know him well enough to place any bets on his likelihood of survival so... I suppose that means I vote yes on contacting Holmes, asking if he would come. If he says no, that's that, and if he says yes, then we'll work with him."

"I agree." Watson bestowed a kiss on my upturned forehead. The tickle of his mustache filled me with such overwhelming gratitude, that it was real, and that we were here together, alive and well and comfortable enough to be a safe harbor for others. I plan to hold him very close tonight. He plans to summon Holmes by telephone first thing in the morning (for Holmes finally had one installed last year).

November 29th 1936

Do you know what that flagrant prat did the moment he arrived? Holmes walked right through our front door without even knocking, came into the sitting room handing off hat, coat, and cane to Watson and I like we were merely the staff at this establishment, assembled his boney self in the seat directly across from Colonel

Hayter, and told him the story of Baron Franz Nopcsa like it would help. Maybe it will, I've seen stranger things perk people out of their own darknesses, but what a reckless gambler Holmes would have been had his life led him down another path. He didn't even pause to read the room, just barreled through and was practically mid-story without so much as a hello and a how-about-this-weather.

Baron Nopcsa began life as a Hungarian-born aristocrat. When his sister discovered the bones of a dinosaur on their Transylvania estate in 1895, he set himself to become a paleontologist, studying those bones and others like it at the University of Vienna. However, he was also an adventurer, which led him to explore the Albanian Alps on foot, to insert himself between tribal disputes to help resolve them, to fight for the freedom of an Albanian nation state, and even to be short-listed as a potential for the first Albanian King. Part of the reason he voted against himself as a possible king was his disinterest in marrying a woman or fathering an heir. Instead he found an Albanian secretary, Bajazid Elmaz Doda, whom Nopcsa immortalized by naming a species of ancient turtle after him, *Kallakobotion bajazidi,* or "beautiful and round Bajazid." Doda became his life-long friend and lover. The phrase 'life-long' is rather key here.

The result of the Great War for Baron Nopcsa was that he was a baron no more. His family's estate was on land ceded to Romania, and he lost all of his possessions, his home, and his place in the world in one fell swoop. He returned with Doda ("the only person who has truly loved me") to Vienna to resume studying fossils and to look for work. A man so brave, energetic, and capable in so many different ways (a polyglot, a spy, a scientist of vision) found poverty to be unbearable and ultimately inescapable. Though it broke his heart to do so, he sold off his personal fossil collection one by one until, profoundly depressed, Nopcsa drugged Doda into a deep sleep and fatally shot him before turning the gun on himself. The note he left behind said, "The reason that I shot my long-time friend and secretary, Mr. Bajazid Elmaz Doda, in his sleep without his suspecting at all, is that I did not wish to leave him behind sick, in misery and without a penny, because he would have suffered too much."

Essentially, Baron Franz Nopcsa was a man of great skill, energy, and fortune (for a time) who nevertheless died at the age of fifty-five from a self-inflicted murder-suicide because the world got him down. This was the story Holmes thought appropriate for Colonel Hayter, a man grieving his gun-shot friend.

Maybe I'm the crazy one. I wouldn't have come in blazing with such a tale, but perhaps Holmes knew something about Hayter from their past interactions that would lead him to believe this sort of tale would engage and not devastate him. However he came to that conclusion, he seemed to be correct.

Colonel Hayter blinked a few times after Holmes's story, and then a wry quirk twisted his mustache. "Hello again, Mr. Holmes," he said.

"Colonel," Holmes said with a nod.

Perhaps it's just one of those things that help men bond, part one-upmanship, part bluff, a dare which asserts that pain doesn't hurt, that loss is nothing, that a man is tough enough to survive anything except maybe himself.

Watson and I left Hayter in the nurturing care of Holmes, for whatever it was worth, to reconvene with each other in the kitchen. We brewed coffee, made a shopping list for our girl Kitty to stock up for our suddenly full house of guests, and cut bread for leftover sandwiches for lunch. As we assembled a pair of trays, drinks on one, food on the other, Watson finally mused about what we'd heard.

"A baron, a paleontologist, a spy, and a freedom fighter," Watson said.

"And almost a king," I added.

"Some people get so much done in so short a time," he said.

"If the price of productivity is burning out sooner, I'll choose being old and lazy," I told him. He pecked me another kiss on the cheek in agreement. I tugged him back to steal a couple more kisses for my lips. I was more ardent than usual with my affection, because there's something about the specter of death that makes one want to live, love, and lust more.

But first it was time for lunch.

Holmes and Hayter were already deep in conversation.

"I'm not saying suicide isn't wrong, it's as wrong as imbibing alcohol, or other harmful substances like *cocaine*," Hayter said, emphasis on the cocaine because of course it was in his house that our Holmes once had a particularly dramatic detoxification, throwing things and being a royal brat about it, or so I've heard. "But I wouldn't go so far as to equate it with murder, as church and state do. A man's life is his own to do with as he sees fit, and some manage it better than others, is all."

"A man's life is not his own," Holmes said. "Each of us is here to serve some sort of purpose. For those who can change the world, they must try, for those who can do little more than suffer, their use is to embody bravery and to set an example for others. Without some sense of service behind being alive, what would stop us all from quitting the business of being alive at the first challenge we met?"

"Do you believe that God has granted us free will?" Hayter countered. "Do you believe in God in the first place, the Christian God?"

"I don't disbelieve what I can't disprove, if that answers your question," he said. "It is logically impossible to prove a negative."

Hayter sighed. "You're about to spin us into theory, and I mean to hold your feet to the ground. Does man have free will, wherever it comes from?"

"He does," Holmes said. "It is his greatest challenge."

"Is there no instance where taking one's own life isn't for the better good? To prevent his own suffering or someone else's?"

Holmes said, "Offering one's life for the sake of another is sacrifice, it is not suicide."

"If sacrificing a life for a life is acceptable to you, then how about a life for a life of comfort? To leave someone an inheritance or to avoid draining their funds with a prolonged illness?"

"What such suffering costs in money it may repay in teaching patience, courage. It may prompt the virtue of charity from others, neighbors or strangers, it may bring a feuding family together for the sake of support. Since it is unknowable what the impact of one person's life, however it is spent, is on the world around them, it is no man's place to remove his life from the pond before his time is up."

"I assume this applies to a woman's life too?" I asked. A man is, does, must, and yet... a man is not a woman.

"Of course," Holmes said, turning his pinpoint glare to me. It's a feeling not unlike getting hit with a light that is focused through a magnifying glass. "Women are kindred close enough to man that they are considered part of mankind. Just as I told the brave, mutilated woman Watson referred to as The Veiled Lodger in his memoirs: your life is not your own, so keep your hands off it."

That was the case of a woman whose face had been mauled off by a circus lion. Watson described her as having "two living and beautiful brown eyes looking sadly out from that grisly ruin" that was her face. She was planning to kill herself with prussic acid, but Holmes told her that her patient suffering was a precious lesson to an impatient world, and that was enough to stay her hand, for a time at least. I doubt either of these men followed-up to see if she didn't choose death in the end.

"Living is easy enough for me to do, personally," I told Holmes. "I have been protected, I have been fortunate, I am happy, I am healthy, and I am accepted for who I am by the people I love." I set my hand on Watson's shoulder. He knows who he is, of course, but he can say the same thing thanks to me, that he is loved for who he is, a man whose devotion is called forth by both men and women. He need not change for me or lie to me, and not every man or woman is as lucky as we.

"You may be somewhat satisfied to know that the Latin, legal name for the crime of self-destruction is without sex, *felo de se* or felon of oneself," Holmes said, smiling because no one would want to celebrate such a thing. "It's a clean reason for the state to take whatever possessions a person has forfeited, regardless of all else."

"How nice to have true equality," I told him.

Colonel Hayter snorted, the closest thing to a laugh he'd emitted in our house. At that moment Watson said we should have music for lunch. He put on a record, and the small sound of a big orchestra intermingled with our chewing and swallowing for the duration of lunch.

Later, Watson took Colonel Hayter on a brisk walk to have some personal time with him, and Holmes silently flipped through our collection of music and flagged a few for my attention.

Without a word, he waved me over to show me each one, and to point to a name: Bessie Smith, Cole Porter, and Lorenz Hart of Rodgers and Hart.

"They aren't all...?" I asked.

"They are, and they're not alone, you and Watson just have a very limited selection."

Good old Sherlock Holmes: on one side, the palm of his hand, a wonder for me to enjoy, and then on the other side, the back of his hand, slapping me with an insult. It was amazing to see.

"Speaking of Harts," he said next, going to inspect the mosaic I'd created around the fireplace, "do you know the name Hart Crane?"

"I... did he write songs too?"

"Poems, most famously 'The Bridge,' as he was inspired by the Brooklyn Bridge in New York."

"As opposed to the one in Marrakesh?" I asked.

Holmes cut his eyes at me but did not engage on that point. I was as much trying to point out that I didn't need everything explained to me while also hoping to distract him from a critical breakdown of my mosaic.

"Crane was a difficult talent to place, to some he was unintelligible, mediocre, without framework, to others he was the new Shelley, an equal to Eliot, a lost son of Whitman. I'm not one for the literary arts, I only wonder if his fixation with the meaning and aesthetic of the Brooklyn Bridge didn't have something to do with how miserable his life was, and how he ultimately died."

I waited, but apparently it was incumbent on me to ask for further information. Holmes wanted his audience to reach for what he was giving.

"How miserable was his life?" I asked. First things first.

"His parents were monstrous," Holmes said. "They were constantly feuding with one another, taking no pains to spare their child from the petty viciousness of adults. Then for his own love life, Crane was prone to seek anonymous sex with rough trade, truck drivers and sailors, men he attempted to educate by reciting poetry at them."

"I bet they loved that," I said. I certainly don't enjoy every repeat lecture I receive from Holmes, but I also never tell him to stop lest I deny myself the new information he has that I want.

"Some of them didn't mind. He lived for a time with a Danish ship's purser named Emil Opffer, and dedicated the poem 'Voyages' to him, but it wasn't enough. He drank heavily, disastrously. He was cut to the bone by bad reviews, and he had plenty of those. He was often arrested for fighting over his bar tabs, and often beat up and robbed when he was out carousing for booze and company. That is what happened on the night he died."

It was now time to ask, "All right, how did he die?" I tried to sound like I was letting Holmes tell me his story, though of course I wanted to hear it. When people bore me, I make excuses to leave. For example, there were dishes I could have cleared sitting right beside me, and I didn't make a single movement towards them, I was intrigued.

"While on board the steamship *Orizaba*, Crane propositioned the wrong crewman and was severely beaten for his troubles. At long last he'd apparently had enough, because he announced, 'Goodbye everybody!' and threw himself overboard."

"And they couldn't fish him out?" I asked.

"His body was never recovered, alive or dead."

"How old was he?"

"Thirty-two," Holmes replied.

"Wow," I said. "Maybe don't tell that story to Colonel Hayter."

"That's why I'm telling you, instead," Holmes informed me, before pointing at my mosaic work and asking, "A garden?"

"Yes!" I had settled on color-clusters like flowers, and was happy my intention was clear. "There's also a mountain, or at least that's how I see it, flowers in the front, a mountain in the distance, pale sky, bright sun."

"I see the mountain," Holmes said, turning back to observe it, hands behind his back, rocking on his feet. "Remember how we included women as part of mankind?"

Oh, it was 'we' now, we were in cahoots.

"I do," I said.

"And you remember the woman who climbed mountains in skirts, a Miss Freda du Faur?"

The Australian mountaineer whom I've loved from afar, though never met or seen, just for being so free, so strong, so bold. The last I knew of her I learned on our trip to Australia in 1921. She had moved to England with her lover Muriel Cadogan. I had hoped to hear of them again, and today I did, from Holmes.

"Her close friend Miss Cadogan suffered a nervous breakdown in 1929," Holmes said. I froze up, knowing this would not end well. "When du Faur checked her into a hospital, they realized this woman wasn't her family, and separated the two women, and contacted Cadogan's family to come retrieve her. They most likely treated her for her illnesses, whatever they believed those were, with electroshock. Cadogan died on the voyage back to Australia, and when du Faur returned home as well and couldn't find any answers as to why her partner had died, she committed suicide by carbon monoxide poisoning just last year, in September."

I tried to speak but only managed a noise before I shivered, not from cold, but from the ghoulishness of the world that was closer than I liked to imagine.

"And how old was Freda?"

"Fifty-two," Holmes said. "If she could have tolerated life for five more days, she would have been fifty-three."

"Are their mountains still theirs?" Mount Du Faur and Mount Cadogan are two of the peaks on New Zealand's South Island, named by Freda after her successful climbs.

"They are," Holmes said. "Touches of immortality that are harder to take away than their lives."

"Right." I sighed. How was I supposed to help Colonel Hayter stay out of the darkness when it was so easy to slip into that space myself?

November 31st 1936

Colonel Hayter has left us. Not 'us' as in 'we the living,' but he has left Chez Watson, and Holmes departed with him, though I don't know how long they'll travel together.

When Watson came back from his walk with Hayter two days ago, it was with a confession to make.

"Darling," he told me when the Colonel was put to bed and Holmes gone off to bunk wherever he was staying, "I need to tell you something."

"Then do so," I told him, wondering why he looked so guilty but largely unconcerned. Watson feels guilty when bad weather foils a nice surprise he was going to give me, so there was a chance he'd done nothing wrong at all.

"Colonel Hayter, he, well..." Watson, at the foot of our bed in his nightclothes, shook his head and looked at the floor. "I'm afraid he kissed me. More than once, and I didn't stop him. In fact, I reciprocated."

A long silence stretched as I figured out how to say what I said next.

"My dear, do you remember the little story Holmes mentioned about Walt Whitman and Oscar Wilde being left alone for a few hours with elderberry wine?"

The non-sequitur surprised my husband. He looked up at me again.

"I... why yes, I do remember that."

"And do you remember he said something along the lines of 'feel free to speculate' about what happened between them?"

"I do," Watson said.

"I did speculate about that," I said, "and I didn't get very far. Remember? I will remind you: Walt Whitman walked the streets looking for working men to spend time with, grown, rough, strong, illiterate men. Oscar Wilde was a twenty-seven-year-old college lad, possibly dressed comically in short pants as was his style for a time, looking tall and soft and much like a young boy who'd been stretched out."

"Right," said Watson, though he did not yet understand where I was headed.

"Meanwhile Oscar Wilde was never so enchanted by anyone as he was by Bosie Douglas, and do you remember what Douglas looked like as a young man? He's rather fair and pretty and boyish even now, in his sixties, whereas Walt Whitman was a grizzled, dirty old man who had probably suffered a stroke by then based on his symptoms. Now tell me, knowing all of that, do you think anything passed between Whitman and Wilde other than wine and words?"

"I suppose I don't," Watson said.

"Neither do I," I told him. "Their natures simply did not match. Now as far as Colonel Hayter is concerned, I think he has always loved you. From the moment you met you've been saving his life, I'd say. You're certainly doing something like that right now, and everything you've ever told me about Hayter has made me guess that he was always hoping you'd feel towards him as you have towards Holmes. But you never did, did you?"

"I mean, I do care for the man, but..."

"But it is only Sherlock Holmes who matches your nature."

"That's right," Watson said. "Darling, I'm so sorry..."

"But you don't have to be," I told him, joining him on the bed and wrapping him in my arms. "I'm not holding you at fault for being lovable, and I'm not upset with Colonel Hayter for loving the man I love myself, I'm barely mad at Holmes about that... anymore. I won't thank him for kissing my husband behind my back, but all things considered, with his friend so recently dead, I dare say he wasn't trying to make a pass at you, was he? He just wanted to be close to someone, and it's no wonder that he'd prefer that someone to be you, because you've always cared for him, just not exactly the way he wished."

Watson was getting sniffly, hugging me back, kissing my neck and tickling me with his mustache.

"You're amazing," he said. "How do you know everything?"

Naturally I don't know everything, even Sherlock Holmes doesn't know that, but I do know my dear Watson well enough. When we went to bed that night, we did not sleep right away.

The next day, yesterday, Colonel Hayter came to breakfast with an announcement.

"Dr. Watson, you've saved me again, truly, but I can't keep taking advantage of your hospitality, wonderful though it's been," he said, nodding to me once before scurrying his eyes away. "Mr. Holmes has done me the honor of inviting me to his seaside home for some fresh air, and I've accepted, I think it may do me well."

"Only repaying an old debt," Holmes said, sipping his morning tea and already dressed to leave.

I must say, so much has come full-circle in one unexpected weekend: Watson to the rescue again, and Holmes offering a home for recovery by mirroring what Hayter had done for him so long ago. I am not so sure that Holmes and Hayter won't rekindle some old flame, though I would bet it's not now and has never been a flame of love, only pure, basic, bodily passion. Still, that's one way to remind oneself that you're alive and you like it. Watson and I were feeling pink and contented for the very same reason.

I was smiling all through my tea and toast, thinking, you know, how do you like that? This time I'm the one Watson wanted to spend a special night with, and it was Holmes who was off with someone else, and everyone seemed fine with it! The novelty, the symmetry of it all, it pleased me then and pleases me now as I write of it.

There was one last departing shot from Holmes, as we all crowded to the door with our chorus of "stay warm" and "drive safely" and "thanks ever so much" and "merry seasons" and all that. He told of George Eastman, founder of the Kodak camera company, father of modern photography, and the inventor of motion picture film.

"If it's fair to say we're all having 'a Kodak moment' we can thank him," said Holmes. "Mr. Eastman lived a long and productive life of wealth and philanthropy. Beneficent to his workers and beloved by many, he never married, and at age seventy-seven shot himself in the heart because, according to a note he left addressed to his friends, 'my work is done—why wait?'"

"That's the big question, isn't it?" Hayter said. "Why wait?"

"Why indeed," said Holmes. "It's up to each of us to answer that for ourselves."

With that, our gentleman callers were gone, off to explore the purpose of life, presumably, and Watson and I were left feeling cuddly towards one another, which is what we spent all yesterday doing, snuggling together in warmth and love.

I think Dorothy Parker put it best in one of her answers to this looming question we all must face, in her poem, "Resumé":

> *Razors pain you;*
> *Rivers are damp;*
> *Acids stain you;*
> *And drugs cause cramp.*
> *Guns aren't lawful;*
> *Nooses give;*
> *Gas smells awful;*
> *You might as well live.*

If the question is why wait to die, my answer is: because it's only a matter of time before we're all done anyway, so why make the effort?

De Amicitia

January 11th 1939

Watson has fallen quite ill, though his spirits stay high. He's more literary than ever when he's delirious with bad health, I've found— he says the bitter winter is quite cooling to a feverish head, and he thinks it would be very neat and fitting to die just before another war breaks out. I don't want him to die, but I don't want either of us to have to live through another war either, and I suppose it's lucky that what I want doesn't matter in any direction: I have no control over my world, only my household, and there are no deathbeds in my house.

January 19th 1939

Watson speaks as if he thinks he's dying, though he's not that bad yet, just sentimental. He's eighty-six years old and doing well at it, though we both agree (when he brings it up) that Sherlock Holmes will outlive him. I have no doubt Holmes could skitter out from under a bomb as mysteriously unscathed as the roaches, but I don't say that to Watson, I merely agree with him that Holmes is steel, he's stern, he's impenetrably healthy and immune to everything but himself. Not at all like my dear Watson, who is soft, sensitive, and so much more susceptible to any passing force.

January 30th 1939

Watson requests that I read to him, stories and poems he remembers from the past. Everything he remembers he wants to talk about, though, so I don't do so much reading as I do listening. I think he just wants to be prompted—his body's unwell but his mind is as sharp as ever, and as a man who has spent his life recording and cataloguing, he wants to make sure he remembers it all just right.

Tonight Watson said, "Holmes always told me his mind rebelled at stagnation; perhaps I've got a bit of that too."

"Every sharp mind hates being dulled," I told him. "Like knives, minds would rather be keen."

"What a keen way to put it," Watson said, and then repeated the word 'keen' several times, savoring its nuances like a flavor.

February 5th 1939

Watson's had me pull down the poetry collection *A Shropshire Lad* to read to him. I don't know why I thought this would be pleasant—I read the poems years ago, they were quite popular among those who wanted the call to war to feel noble and worthy, but I'd forgotten the tone of them. Perhaps the flower on the cover and the idea of country lads from a time before the Great War put me in some halcyon idyll, but I was expecting to read some simple, pleasant verses about meadows and larks and the sweet sorrows of youth. Though the rhymes are neat and the meadows present, the poems are full of loss and death at every turn. It is not something I would have picked to read to a dying man, but it's not my deathbed, and I still doubt it's Watson's either. Until it's time to bar the priest from the door, this is a sickbed to me and nothing more morbid than that.

Of course, reading poems about journeys ending does nothing to help morale. I can barely understand why they make Watson so happy.

February 14th 1939

Happy Valentine's Day! The mystery is revealed: Watson tells me that the author of the poems (an A.E. Housman, who died a few years ago of exceedingly old age, though he died younger than my Watson is today), spent his life in love with a friend he met in university, and that all these poems about soldiers, athletes, and travelers come from that devotion. All the poems about suicide and longing and guilt and unrequited love? They come from that place, too.

Speaking of that kind of love, Watson cannot help but talk of Sherlock Holmes. If Holmes thinks Watson's stories are too revealing and florid (and I know for a fact that he does), he should hear Watson chatter on and on about him when he's out of the room—he's a frightful gossip. Certainly that's something I love about him, the way he talks, and the way we talk together.

Never forget that St. Valentine was killed for marrying lovers in secret.

February 26th 1939

We've finished the *Shropshire* poems and moved to Housman's other collection, *Last Poems*. Watson tells me they were published just before Housman's great friend from university died. Watson and I agree that was no coincidence.

March 8th 1939

We've finished reading the poems of Housman, but Watson hasn't requested we start another book. Today he told me just about everything he's heard about A.E. Housman:

"I've managed to meet his brother a few times, Laurence Housman, and though the poet Housman was rather famously reticent, Laurence certainly wasn't. Holmes knew him better than

I ever did, maybe that's why Laurence talked so freely—Holmes was always in the room with us, and he's a great secret-keeper. Apparently, according to Laurence, Alfred" (that's A.E.) "sent a copy of his poems to Oscar Wilde after his release from prison, which I think was rather... sweet?" Watson asked.

"Bittersweet," I answered.

"Yes, that's it exactly. It's understandable; what happened to Oscar Wilde had an effect on all of us."

All of them, he means: men of a certain affection. It prompted Holmes to relapse into cocaine use, according to Watson's old diaries and memories. It put a strain on their partnership, their relationship, their life together (for a while at least, as they were off and on for years).

Watson continued. "Housman spent years in the Patent Office as a clerk, even though he was clearly an eminent Latin scholar. He went through Oxford, did all the work to earn the degree, but when it came time to sit for the final exams, he just... didn't do them. He sat, but he hardly wrote anything. He never told his brother any particular reason why, but their father had just fallen very ill, so that may well have done it. Regardless, he didn't pass his exams, and he couldn't retake them for any reason."

I harrumphed a bit at that. I've been a teacher, and absolutely despise seeing schools work against students instead of for them. Watson smiled to hear that noise.

"You and Holmes have shared the same rant on schools," he said in teasing—he knows I prickle at being too much like the 'other man' in his life. "You know Holmes was an independent student, only learned what he felt was worth knowing and practically unlearned anything he found useless to him particularly."

"Yes," I said. "He refused to learn everything but still acts as if he knows it all."

Watson smiled again and continued. "So A.E. Housman took the Civil Service exam—that one he passed very sufficiently—and that good friend of his, named Moses if you can believe it, had a position with the Civil Service too!"

"What a coincidence!"

"Isn't it though! Laurence Housman said his brother turned down a first job offer in Ireland because Moses was not in Ireland, and the next job let him move in with the Jackson brothers for a few years of... not exactly happiness. Moses never loved him back the same way. His younger brother did though."

"Really? Housman got involved with his true love's brother?"

"According to his own brother, not that they ever spoke of such things, of course."

"Of course, not in those days."

"Not much in these days either. Laurence Housman bravely and publically advocates for better, but..."

I nodded. That was all we could really say about that.

March 12th 1939

Watson has written a lengthy letter to Holmes (or rather he dictated and I wrote) telling him about his ill health and asking him about the Housman brothers, since now his curiosity is stimulated. My husband is a compulsive story-teller, he can't help himself: he doesn't know enough about the poet Housman to feel satisfied, and though that poet has recently died out of an extremely reclusive and secretive life, if anyone might have any unrecorded details about him, it would be the world's most famous consulting detective.

April 1st 1939

April Fools—our housekeeper Kitty convinced me that I had a stain on the back of my dress for nearly ten straight minutes while I strained to look over my shoulder at a mirror. I tricked Watson into thinking it was the first of May (mayday, mayday!), though the joke was on me, as Watson only wondered why Holmes had not yet answered his letter.

April 12th 1939

Holmes's response has arrived, with a wrapped book. I read the letter to Watson this morning while he opened the book like it was a Christmas present.

> *My dear Watson,*
> *I'm sorry to hear you're unwell. I'll tell you a few stories, my friend, in the hopes that it will cheer you up and out of bed (and for the snooping gaze of Mrs. Watson, whom I'm sure will read this letter before it even reaches your bedside table).*

I glanced up at Watson after reading that jab. Watson shrugged, but smiled at me, so I continued reading.

> *If you're interested in what Laurence Housman has to say about his brother, I've included a book published quite recently, a remembrance by LH of AEH, stories from their childhood, a few letters, and some rather pithy criticisms of just about anyone the poet was asked to expound upon. But I have more details for you than are fit to be published.*
> *LH informed me that his brother died with a very thorough collection of banned and pornographic literature—the only proof that AEH had been the owner of those pages is that he corrected all of the grammar mistakes and misprints by hand.*

Watson snorted to hear that. I too had to twist a smirk off my face before I could continue reading.

> *I met AEH once—I was at Cambridge on unrelated business, and happened to know he took regular walks over the grounds. Having known his brother, I was curious to observe the recluse, but he was reclusive for a reason; he did not want to be observed. I would say he was nearly*

as unclubbable as my own brother, Mycroft—some men don't want to be known or recognized, they don't want to be famous.

I said, "Ugh, none of the men I know," which I am happy to report made Watson laugh harder than anything Holmes had written in his letter.

On the second day, as I watched AEH walking across the grounds of Cambridge, he halted and looked me in the eye and said, "Stop spying on me!" I was in disguise and tried to deny the accusation, but he insisted he'd seen me watching him the day before, that I was a fraud and certainly wasn't the scholar I was dressed as.

"In my career I've known many frauds hiding behind books in the academy."

I straightened my posture and removed the odds and ends I'd glued to my face for disguise and introduced myself.

"I'm Sherlock Holmes."

"I recognize you now. You're drawn quite a bit better than I ever am."

I nodded. "I'm not on any case, I'm only curious. I know your brother, Laurence."

"Knowing my brother Laurence is no introduction to me."

"Laurence told me you'd say something like that, if you didn't want to have the trouble of talking to me."

AEH snorted then, hard enough to disturb his mustache, but he didn't walk away. I'd managed to amuse him slightly by being so frank. Another man who'd stayed in the rooms across from him once had forgotten to pack his own trousers, and had to ask AEH to borrow a pair out of shameless necessity, despite the man's reputation—he even had to ask for permission to split them up the back, so they would fit!

That man was tolerated too, for surprising AEH so well; he hated to be disturbed by dullards.

We started to wander very slowly in each other's orbit. I proceeded to point out some of the plants along the path to make conversation. He's quite an avid cataloger of local flora, and I started guessing incorrectly so that I could give every plant some vile name—I did this because LH told me his brother had a wicked sense of humor, if properly provoked, and a bit of correct Latin would go an even greater distance with the professor. So I said to him, "Over there I see one that looks like a Phallus amorphous, *but it appears it hasn't come up yet."*

"Perhaps modesty forbids?" AEH conjectured in his attractive, thin mandarin voice. Neither one of us laughed, amusing though it was. We were circling each other at this point, rather mutually suspicious—we both knew more than we were saying, but neither of us would speak its name.

"I know many people I respect who greatly admire your poems," I told him, mostly speaking of you, Watson, as you've always been one for poetry.

AEH responded with, "I've always liked your dismissal of literature as irrelevant to your true, scientific work."

"You must have read that about me in Watson's stories," I said, "and aren't they literature?"

"I've liked detective stories since I was a boy, I never quite matured away from them."

"We all have shameful habits from our youths," I agreed. He glared at me for pointing that out, but I was including myself quite plainly, so he let it go.

I interrupted the letter with, "Wait—how well does Holmes know Laurence Housman, are they friends, or are they...?"

"Intimate friends," Watson said with a nod. "I would assume so, though we've never talked about it specifically, obviously."

"I guess it runs in families sometimes? Both Housman brothers preferred the company of men."

"Laurence actually enjoys the *company* of women," Watson said. "He supports women's rights and counts many women as friends, but his brother could count the amount of women he found tolerable on one hand, I hear, and besides that I know what you mean. There are more than two Housman brothers, if that helps explain it, and a couple of sisters too. With enough siblings, statistically, it would have to happen sometimes, wouldn't it?"

"More often than we'd ever admit in public, that is sure," I said.

"You had seven brothers before the war, darling, did you ever wonder about any one of them? Or maybe two of them?"

I nodded to Watson. I had thought about it, especially after learning that Watson and Holmes had often been more than what they appeared to be towards one another during their years at Baker Street. About one brother particularly I could easily be convinced, the second youngest, my brother William. He was hardly old enough, in my mind, to be anything but a baby, but of course he was old enough to be a soldier in a uniform, old enough to die on the battlefield, as was the fate written about in so many of A.E. Housman's poems. So certainly he was old enough to have loves, and secrets, and a whole life to himself that I would never have known about.

I returned to Sherlock Holmes's letter feeling more somber.

> *Another friend of AEH's, who knew him later in life around the time when I met him, noticed his face always lapsed into a mien of sadness when he wasn't engaged. That man's Mrs. (like most wives, like yours) said with a nearly correct intuition, "That man has had a tragic love affair!" She was correct, but it was not a love for a lady that put that feeling into AEH's features—what that woman's husband said was that it was like some other poet's phrase, 'sad as mortality.' Sometimes poets do know what they're talking about. That*

fellow is writing a book about AEH too, you should find it if you're still interested after reading the one I've included. It should publish by next year.

I smiled a bit to myself at that idea. Holmes, for how little he and I get along, still share one goal in common: keeping Watson. Keeping him alive, and happy, and keeping him jealously from one another as often as we can. Watson now has a reason to insist on living—he will most certainly want to read that next book, he can't leave a story unfinished.

> *AEH did not take to friends or even casual companions easily, and he and I parted rather stiffly.*
>
> *"I don't want to see you snooping around about me after today," he said as we'd come to the edge of the college grounds and he planned to continue on through more bucolic terrain without company.*

Alone in Arcadia always, that man.

> *"I don't suppose you could stop me if I disregarded your preference for privacy?" I asked him. I admit I was being difficult, but I was speaking with an evenly matched opponent in the difficulty department. "You may have heard, I've battled a professor before, and I won."*
>
> *"Barely won," AEH said. "It was quite easy for us all to believe you were dead for a few years, almost as if the world expected you to fail."*
>
> *"We'll call this battle a stalemate, then, shall we?" I asked.*
>
> *"Call it what you want, just don't record it anywhere, and hold Dr. Watson to that as well—I'd never speak a word to him, not an ounce of discretion in his whole body, he's as indiscreet as an American with how much he tattles." AEH walked away from me after that, and I never followed him again.*

He was correct in his assessment of you, Watson, you naturally repel secrets and you love to tell tales, but he was right to suspect me as well; I've just disregarded his request by penning this missive, haven't I?

Warm regards,

Sherlock Holmes

P.S. I've also included LH's address if you'd like to write him for more information—I hear he's composing an essay on his brother's relationship with that great friend, that Moses Jackson. It won't be public or published for some time, but I'm sure he'll tell you about it if you ask him while mentioning my name—he knows how close we've been.

May 4th 1939

Watson was out of bed like a shot after receiving that letter. Holmes had given him an assignment, and suddenly that small bit of work gave him an invigorating purpose. I took down all the things he noted to me while reading the Laurence Housman book, but it was mostly Latin to me until he let out a very scandalized gasp of recognition, and started to laugh a much courser laugh than is natural to him. I came to the study to find him at his desk, both hands on the book propped up in front of him, and his head thrown back with a full-throated guffaw. It was the laugh of a man who had an answer very few people could even hope to grasp. Sherlock Holmes laughs like that, but hardly ever my Watson.

I asked him what fresh detail had been revealed, afraid for a moment that he might dismiss me as being incapable of understanding, but it was only that unfamiliar laugh that made me doubt him. Watson explained it to me quite quickly.

"Among his brother's papers, Laurence found a copy of a book by another Lawrence, T.E. Lawrence."

"Lawrence of Arabia, our conquering hero." I remembered how enshrined he was after the Great War, coming back from faraway lands sunburnt but unbroken, a success when so many others had failed or fallen.

"Did you ever read his book about the Arab campaign?"

"Absolutely not." It was one thing to feel a bit of national pride for his return to England, but coming from such a soldier-filled family that was completely demolished (save myself) after the war, nothing would interest me in reading the story of a lengthy military operation.

"I did," Watson said, turning to me and handing me this Housman book. "A.E. Housman did too, and he made a note in his copy, look at what his brother says here."

> *What Alfred thought about himself in his personal relations has been written for him by another. In* Seven Pillars of Wisdom *T.E. Lawrence gives the following introspective account of himself:*
>
> *'There was my craving to be liked—so strong and nervous that never could I open myself friendly to another. The terror of failure in an effort so important made me shrink from trying; besides, there was the standard; for intimacy seemed shameful unless the other could make the perfect reply, in the same language, after the same method, for the same reasons.*
>
> *'There was a craving to be famous; and a horror of being known to like being known. Contempt for my passion for distinction made me refuse every offered honour...'*
>
> *Against this passage, Alfred wrote in the margin, 'This is me.'*

There was the beginning of a tear in my eye by the end of that page, but I tried to 'soldier on' past sympathy by saying, "Well, see, I told you all men want to be famous."

Watson laughed and then said, "Shall I tell you what's whispered about Lawrence of Arabia?"

"Please do!" I said. I thought it would lighten the mood to know more behind-closed-doors secrets, but it did not.

"First of all," Watson began, pulling the behemoth of *Seven Pillars of Wisdom* from the bookshelf and opening it to the beginning, "read the dedication."

I did. It's a bit of a poem dedicating the book to an S.A. that begins:

> *I loved you, so I drew these tides of*
> *Men into my hands*
> *And wrote my will across the*
> *Sky and stars*
> *To earn you freedom, the seven*
> *Pillared worthy house,*
> *That your eyes might be*
> *Shining for me*
> *When I came*

I had nothing to say to that, and Watson spoke on.

"S.A. was most likely an Arab boy Lawrence was rather fond of, and he also pointed out in this book once or twice that in the desert men and boys loved each other quite freely sometimes, honestly, and without shame."

"No wonder he was so restless back home, if that's something he admired."

"No wonder at all," said Watson.

I do know that our Lawrence of Arabia changed his name after it became famous, partly to rid himself of that distinguished and official admiration (he really must have preferred being liked to being famous), and partly to join back up in the Royal Air Force in the lower ranks, so he could have company rather than stiff, remote authority. Certainly fame and intimacy aren't the same forms of attention.

All I said to Watson about these thoughts was, "I know he changed his name to rejoin the Royal Air Force in disguise, that was so odd when it was found out."

"Not when you take into consideration another moment in *Seven Pillars* where he writes of being captured in Deraa, then questioned, beaten, and sexually abused by his captors."

"How horrible!" I said.

"Well..." Watson began, hesitating. "He didn't write about it as if it were entirely horrible. There are several men I know who swear he made up the story, that the Bey he named as his abuser was not at all known for that sort of treatment of men."

"Why would Lawrence of Arabia make up such a thing?"

Watson flipped to another page he'd marked in *Seven Pillars* and read to me, "'I remembered the corporal kicking with his nailed boot to get me up; and this was true, for next day my right side was dark and lacerated, and a damaged rib made each breath stab me sharply. I remembered smiling idly at him, for a delicious warmth, probably sexual, was swelling through me: and then that he flung up his arm and hacked with the full length of his whip into my groin.'"

"Heavens," was all I could think to say to that. It would have been more appropriate to say, "Hell."

"It says he was used first by the underguards, rejected by the Bey for being too battered for his bed, and that after this refusal the youngest and most beautiful of the corporals had to stay with the Bey instead, while Lawrence was tossed out into the cold."

"It still might have happened, regardless of the Bey's reputation, perhaps?" I asked. And despite such a tender rendering of it as nearly erotic? Though I didn't mention that idea.

Watson grimaced a bit. His sordid tale was not finished.

"When T.E. Lawrence returned home to England," Watson said, "and this is something very few people know—I only heard it from Colonel Hayter, who heard it from another man once removed from the true story—but upon return to England, Lawrence of Arabia is said to have hired fellow service men to whip him while he exercised. One even said that Lawrence insisted on Beethoven being played while the whippings took place, and another said these lashings were something he needed to endure before asking to be... conquered. Penetrated. Regardless, apparently he had a rather intricate, unlikely story about this treatment being imposed on him by an uncle. He wrote letters of instruction on the punishment he should receive in the guise of this uncle, and he was doing this right up until he died on that motorcycle of his."

After some silence I said, "I doubt A.E. Housman has any stories like that."

"As do I," Watson said, turning back to his book. "I get the impression that he would listen to stories like that quite closely, though."

It's hard to hold such curiosity against anyone. I wouldn't plug up my ears if offered more details either, they certainly draw the mind.

May 29th 1939

Watson sent a letter to Laurence Housman. Though I don't know what his letter said, I know it was lengthy (felt its density when I asked Kitty to post it), and Mr. Housman has answered it with much the same length and detail. Watson still feels in good health, and has since the day this interest seized him at Holmes's command. In fact, he was in such high spirits that he did the hard work of squinting through his glasses for the pleasure of reading the letter to me instead of having me read it to him.

> *Hello Dr. Watson,*
>
> *I do indeed remember our brief meetings, though I must say I feel somewhat more familiar with you than those moments can justify—I've simply gleaned so much of you from your stories, and from the corrections our friend Sherlock likes to make of them whenever he's asked if they're true.*
>
> *I'm glad you enjoyed the book about my brother. He was a reticent chap even with his own family, but as I know from talking with the few friends he allowed himself to have, there was so much depth to him that he never wanted to let on*

about, and certainly no one person was allowed to view but a tip of that iceberg.

I was surprised, for example, that he'd been so bold as to send A Shropshire Lad *to Oscar Wilde. I sent Wilde a book of mine too, having met him once before his misfortune (it arrived the same day as my brother's in a coincidence that Wilde mentioned when he thanked me in a letter, saying it gave him a brief moment of rare happiness). Mr. Wilde once complimented me by borrowing a sentence of mine he found beautiful for his* The Picture of Dorian Gray, *and so I sent him everything I wrote for commentary until he died—I'm sure my brother would have too, had he written as many books as I have, or perhaps not; Wilde won a prize for poetry at Oxford that my brother tried for later and lost, and my brother wouldn't have forgotten that. He also found most of Wilde's poetry unexceptional... except for the last one, the "Ballad of Reading Gaol," though he did wonder to me if Alfred Douglas didn't write the better parts of it.*

"Outrageous!" I said, knowing as much as can be known about Oscar Wilde's scandalous misfortune. "When Douglas is the reason he went to prison in the first place! He isn't half the poet of any of the others."

"Laurence agrees with you, darling, let me finish," Watson said before reading on.

I think my brother was teasing me by writing that—I knew Wilde's truer friend Robbie Ross quite a bit better, and he kept himself in between Douglas and Wilde as much as he could, though he couldn't keep them apart altogether. One cannot help the color of one's hair, to badly quote my brother, and certainly one cannot take back a heart given too freely ('give crowns and pounds and guineas, but not your heart away'!). In fact, my brother could have taken some credit for what he deemed an improvement of Wilde's poetics—Ross memorized several of Alfred's poems and recited them to Oscar Wilde while he was still in prison. I'm thinking of one that, just like Wilde's "Ballad of Reading Gaol," is about a criminal soon to be hanged. That one was also used by a famous American barrister in a case of two young, rather intimately involved murderers—he took a measure of credit for saving Leopold and Loeb from the hangman's noose... why not feel flattered by Wilde's ballad of love, lies, and loss?

I'm writing a truer account of my brother now, and of his hidden nature. He gave me the option as his executor to burn, censor, or otherwise destroy that poem he wrote on Oscar Wilde's conviction ('Who is that young sinner'), but if he'd have wanted it burned he would have done it himself. One of his poems praises a young man who killed himself rather than let his kind of love bring shame upon him and his family ('Shot? So quick, so clean an ending?'), and how could I let that be my brother's last word on the matter when even he could not burn out his own true feeling? He wanted to say more in his life, but if it can only be recorded after his death, so be it. I believe that every bit of kindness and understanding helps. My brother once wrote, 'The toil of all that be helps not the primal fault; It rains into the sea, and still the sea is salt.' However, if he wanted to believe that to the end, he'd have known better than to leave any of his sensitive material to me.

I'm going to call this revelatory essay 'De Amicitia'—Latin to honor my brother's trade, the original Romance language—which for us English translates to 'On Friendship.' He kept Moses Jackson's portrait at the top of those cold, remote steps in Cambridge to the end of his days. When I asked him who that man was (the one time I was ever allowed into my brother's rooms), his voice deepened and he said, "That was my friend

Jackson, the man who had more influence on my life than anyone else." Beside that portrait was another one, Adalbert Jackson, Moses's younger brother. They three lived together after he left Oxford in disgrace for the Civil Service, and while I still think there was more mutual attraction between him and Moses, it wasn't enough. Moses shied away from the full implication, knowing he could not share it 'in kind.' But (and this is what I want you to realize): his attraction to the younger brother was reciprocated. I doubt whether Moses ever kissed Alfred: but I have no doubt that Adalbert did, and in fact I have no doubt whatever that my brother was in closer and warmer physical relationship with Adalbert than with Moses. But Adalbert died of typhoid unexpectedly, and Moses moved far abroad and married, and so my brother was left to his work, and to those poems he considered a self-immolation, almost too painful to acknowledge (let alone write), but he wrote them to give to his friend, and he'd willingly suffer that and more for his friend—he made that clear enough with all that he did.

Not all bad though—I told Sherlock and I'll tell you the same, Alfred was quite funny when he had reason to be. I've seen my brothers bent double laughing at Alfred's letters, and someone in Adalbert's family saw him do the same, said he nearly fell out of his chair once. That part of Alfred's reputation was well-known enough that the last thing the doctor said to him before letting him go from this world was an inappropriate story. Alfred laughed and said the doctor's joke was so good he'd be telling it on the Golden floor the next day. To whom he would be speaking in the afterlife specifically he didn't say, though it would be easy to guess... but then again, he was also an atheist, speaking in metaphor only.

If you're inclined I would be interested in your commentary on the essay before I turn it over to the British Museum—

neither of us will see it published I'm afraid, so it's help edit or never know! The instruction will be to keep it under lock and key for twenty-five years.

Send my regards to Sherlock—I hope we see each other again.
-Laurence Housman

Watson lowered the letter and sighed. "Twenty-five years."

"Maybe the world will be different enough by then," I said.

Enough is changing all the time; finish one war to wait for another, punish one man for what the future will know is love, and all the while one's own life falls on the timeline wherever it lands, and we make the best of it.

"I wonder if I ever met Moses Jackson in India," Watson said. "I might have, for all I know, though I don't remember meeting anyone so captivating that he'd inspire a lifetime of devotion."

I smiled at Watson. This from the man who thinks Sherlock Holmes may truly be immortal, who has done his best to preserve his dear friend in writing, though it's pained him over and over again. He doesn't regret a single day of their partnership—not even the blackest of days when he and Holmes fought, or injured, or dismissed one another—as that would only mean losing a part of the whole picture. I can't think of anyone who could understand A.E. Housman's heart better than my dear Watson.

I quoted him a bit of Housman's verse to remind him of that fact, and left him with a kiss on his cheek knowing that tomorrow was another step into the future we'd continue to meet together:

But if you come to a road where danger
Or guilt or anguish or shame's to share,
Be good to the lad that loves you true
And the soul that was born to die for you,
And whistle and I'll be there.

About the Author

L.A. Fields is the author of two Lambda Literary Award finalists, five YA books, one short story collection, and two works of scholarship. She has an MFA and a calico cat.

www.ingramcontent.com/pod-product-compliance
Lightning Source LLC
Chambersburg PA
CBHW051257250626
47155CB00009B/3328